JIMMY'S FACE

MEETS

BRICK WALL

JIMMY'S FACE MEETS BRICK WALL

A story by Fapelo

Onaleye Pelumi Favour

WORDS
RHYMES &
RHYTHM

Printed and Published in Nigeria by:
Words Rhymes & Rhythm Limited
Suite C309, Global Plaza Plot 366, Obafemi
Awolowo Way, Jabi District, Abuja, Nigeria.
08169027757, 08060109295
www.wrr.ng

DEDICATION

To the one that made this possible.
To the wolf pacque.
To puzzles.
To family.

CONTENTS

About Fapelo

I have a question for you.
Have you ever been in a situation
where you are totally blindsided and have no
idea how things got the way they were?
You were doing something in order to
get some other thing, but then out of nowhere,
one whole other thing you never considered is
what you get.
There you were, in wherever you were
where this unexpected outcome hits you in the
face like a ton of bricks, looking how Tom
looked when he figured out that his new
resident rat neighbor – Jerry, knew nuclear
physics.
Well, that's the way I feel right now
writing this bio, because I just realized that
the bio I am writing is going to fit right into
the prologue of a short story I am working on.
So I wondered '...is that how really
like my characters I am?'
If so, then if you truly want to know
me, read all my works both recent, old,
complete and incomplete. Try to decipher that
key message hidden between the lines about
who this peculiar author is.
Bon Appetite! BUHAHAHA! "Okay,
that was a little too much."

AUTHOR'S PROLOGUE – ABOUT MY CRUSH

It was Saturday night at the rotary's bar, and way past the time that any churchgoing fella should be found in such establishments.

Three friends sat around the most unused table in the bar, like the knights of the roundtable.

The bar was a fancy one, its drinks were way overpriced but it had just the right kind of clientele.

They each had a shot of drink in their respective fronts and there roughly around the center of the table sat a large bottle of the most alcoholic drink the bar could offer.

They usually did this ritual almost every month on a Saturday night like this. They gathered at this particular spot to talk, but it was not really just that they never saw each other before their ragtag meetings. It was just that most men tended to talk more loosely under the influence of Alcohol.

Usually, they just reveled in each other's misfortunes and tease themselves about the other's successes.

This particular Saturday night though, none of the usual banter was taking place.

The most dominant sound in the bar that moment was the clink of glasses as the bartender cleaned the glass mugs and replaced them in their respective cases.

There on that table at the center of the bar, these three non-churchgoing fellows sat and fixed all their attention on one thing.

What could enrapture three men so much so that not a word was being uttered by a single one of them?

It was an android phone, better yet it was the picture of the girl splayed elegantly on the display of the aforementioned phone.

Not just any girl though, but the new assistant of one of these three gentlemen.

It was the shortest of the three that broke the silence, "This is Toyin?" he asked.

His question was directed at the fella sitting across from him –he had a gentle face and a pronounced body. The fella he asked smiled and said, "Yes, Tim that is Toyin, my new assistant."

"Duuuuuude!" Tim said, drawing it out as long as possible.

Their other companion who had been silent up till then said as if he had just come to a major realization; "Hmm... makes sense..."

He raised his fingers to his temples and began to bob his head up and down like a particular math problem just got solved in his head.

He was the prettiest of the trio though he lacked the attractive dominant physique of his friend and housemate Jimmy.

"… All those late nights, I thought you were already taking your job seriously." He continued, "I should have known that nothing short of a woman could get it into that pretty boy head of yours to take your work seriously"

Andrew – the fella who just spoke, was a photographer and he worked for a magazine owned by his father. His friend Jimmy also worked for his father. Jimmy was a model and though he sometimes took external commissions, he basically was an employee of his roommate's dad.

"Guys…." Said Jimmy he had a sad smile on his face, "I think I am in love."

The other two couldn't quite believe their ears when they heard this, Andrew's amused laughter echoed across the almost empty bar. Tim glanced at the hot drink in his front and put on a mock worried face, grabbed it and took a swig.

Tim being the dramatic one stood up and said "Hol' up… wait a freaking second, weren't you the one that was saying about a week ago that *batface* was gonna drop you because you were her youngest client?"

Batface was the nickname the three of them adapted for Jimmy's former middle-aged assistant because of her looks and also that little odd nag that she looked more alive at night time.

"So..." said Andrew finishing Tim's question, "...how does a guy that had no assistant end up with one – a very pretty one at that, in so short a time?"

Tim grabbed his chair and dragged it towards Jimmy, he sat down and fixed him with an expression that showed total attentiveness, "Spare no detail!" he said.

"Well..." he said as if he was scrambling to figure out where to start his tale from then his eyes lit up like he suddenly had an idea.

He fixed a crooked foxy smile on his face and said to his friends. "You have to say the story pledge!" He crossed his arms like that was the deal breaker and he leaned back to watch his friends.

The *story pledge* was a drunken fabrication of the three pals –one they took seriously. They basically invented a pledge to a mock god –*Interruptus*. To them, *Interruptus* was a Greek philosopher and god, whose sole purpose was to prevent stories from being interrupted.

So, the lawyer amongst the trio – Tim, came up with a short pledge that they usually recited before any of them told a story to prevent interruptions during tales.

They came with this idea because most nights before the pledge they usually easily got off topic and never really finished telling their individual stories.

Anyone who broke the pledge had to take two straight shots of the drink that was a constant guest in their meetings.

Andrew and Jimmy exchanged a quick glance and they both in unison leaned back and raised their left palm outwards and their right palms as though to cover their mouths but stop a hair short leaving enough room for their lips to move freely and they began to together chant not losing rhythm;

"O lord Interruptus.

I pledge to be a loyal listener.

To keep all jokes and puns pending

And drench all unholy Inquisitions,

In thy holy liquor"

Jimmy cleared his throat, he was still smiling because he knew his friends would still interrupt.

"Andrew knows this part of the story, I ran into her on Monday and recognized her. She was my junior sister's best friend when they were kids." He began, "When I saw her, she seemed to be preoccupied with walking as fast as she could –almost like she was running away from something. I very much suspected from the expression plastered all over her face, that if she didn't care at all about the attention it was gonna draw she might have flat out run. She was exiting the Reebok building down at marina when we bumped into each other literally – if we hadn't I don't think I would have taken the moment to really look at her." Jimmy paused like he was actually reminiscing.

"I realized who she was but it took me another minute to recall her name, as I recalled her name was Toyin I turned to call her name to see her outline receding in the peripheral of my right eye. I remember thinking to myself 'For such a slight woman she sure moves fast' I don't know what came over me but I just began to chase after her." He continued, "I rounded the bend she just took to see that she had vanished from sight. I walked further forward to see if there were any other ways she could have gone and I found none."

"Resigned to the fate that I won't see her again I turned to return to my destination, I was actually there to see another lady for the assistant job. I suddenly felt a very sharp object poke me in the spine – apparently, I had missed a small conspicuous spot that could just fit a lady of her size.

She cleared her throat loudly and asked me why I was following her, I don't know what happened to me but at that moment a newspaper headline flashed before me 'Male model stabbed to death opposite the Reebok building.'"

He gently demonstratively raised his arms up in the form of surrender as trying to replicate his next action in his story.

"Slowly and gently I raised both my arms in surrender and explained myself to her that I was Tanya's brother," he resumed, "I heard her voice quiver like she was fighting back tears as she told me to turn around slowly. As I turned I saw that she was holding a metal scrap with a wicked looking edge. As soon as I turned fully I saw her expression change to one of pure anguish, she released the metal and let it fall to the ground as she tackled me into a very sudden tight hug. Tears fell freely from her eyes."

"Wait a minute...." Andrew interrupted and winced.

"You never mentioned the hug...... all you said was that you guys had dinner together." He garbled out as he took two shots of drink, "Plus, you also failed to mention how hot she was."

"Well, at first..." Jimmy continued smiling at his friend "I was blind, to say the least, and I didn't see her in that way. We left the marina and went to that suya spot at Leriake's Joint. We used one of their inner booths. She told me about what had been going on in her life and I began to understand why she looked so miserable. According to what she told me that day, her father was an asshole that owed a lot of big men a lot of money. He owed one in particular so much money that in order to soothe his dwindling patience he promised his only daughter to him, she was seven when this occurred. So along the line, as she grew, this man visited occasionally but he never stayed for more than an hour, he paid for all her schooling and clothes and other miscellaneous stuff. She got used to seeing him and answering precarious and awkward questions about her personal life. This happened until when she left home to study in the university – which he also paid for as well. The rich man fell sick and requested for her presence, this was the first time he had called for her. He told her he knew he was dying and he felt bad about how he had agreed to such a deal with her father..." He paused again like he was trying to remember something.

He suddenly snapped his fingers like he had gotten it, then continued the story, "...Oh, I forgot at this point her father was already dead for like two years. The rich dude told her he would continue to sponsor her till she graduated, but he expected nothing of her. She had left for school the next day only to find out a few days later that the rich dude had died not long after she left."

"She said that she had only a year left and she had been saving up for a while, so she could afford to pay her tuition herself for that last year, but before she did, she found out that someone already did. She went back home for the man's funeral and she was approached by the man's son, she called him Dare. Apparently, his father had made him swear that he was going to continue to cater for her before he died."

"Ermm... Jimmy I know I said spare no details but when are we getting to the good stuff" Tim said as he took a shot then another.

Ironically being the only lawyer amongst the trio and the one that came up with the rules, he sure broke *interruptus* rule more than any other.

"Well... if you hadn't interrupted, right about now. Fast-forward to the beginning of this month, our girl just got back from service and was interning at the Reebok Pharmaceutical institute –the one located at the three top floors of the Reebok building."

"Chill... Hold on... Your girl's a Pharmacist?"

I nodded

"...when that Dare dude who was somewhat of a crime lord at this point, paid her a visit and informed her that it was either she got married to him or she paid back every kobo his father spent on her. She had pleaded with him that she would pay him back as soon as possible but he ignored her pleas and he sent men to seize her company issued vehicle, that was last week. This week though she became very paranoid, she felt she was being followed everywhere and she started shacking up with one of her former course mates back at the university."

"So, correct me if I am wrong here Jimmy," Andrew said "you decided to offer her a job, the good Samaritan that you are"

"Yep, but that happened another day," Jimmy answered miming a hand motion for drink and gesturing at the bottle, "that day all I did was listen and be a good friend and of course I gave her the number of the most badass person I knew?"

"You have Vin Diesel's personal number?" Tim asked, somewhat sarcastically. He raised his hand in mock surrender as he snatched the bottle from Andrew who just finished pouring his second shot and took a swig straight out of the bottle.

"No, remember that private detective I told you that helped my sister out when she had that nasty *'My boyfriend won't take a hint'* situation," Jimmy asked him.

"Yea...yea that dude with the black weird-looking beat-up Volvo.... Ajala something" Tim said swinging the bottle back and forth obviously way buzzed than his friends were.

"Ajayi..." Jimmy corrected "I gave him a call and asked for a favor. He asked me to tell him the whole story so I gave her the phone and let her tell the story herself. I went to the Suya-bar to get something for myself and her to go – when I returned she was positively beaming with a very cute smile, one I have come to find endearing in the past couple of days. I was very surprised to see this smile but more so that she was done with the call very quickly. When I asked what about just happened and why she was smiling, she told me that Ajayi just told her that the cops just arrested Dare –the thug. It was apparently all over the news. She was still beaming at this point and I joined as I heard this news. 'Splendid!', I remembered saying. 'So,' I had continued, 'You can go back to your normal life now?'. She then replied and said that Ajayi had told her to lay low for a couple months so that everybody involved will forget about her. We left the Suya spot half an hour later and I had her dropped off at her friend's place. I stared at her for a moment in the illumination of the porchlight when I was saying Goodbye, it was already dark at this point and I think that was when I knew it, I was hooked guys."

"So let me get this straight," Andrew said, "You didn't ask her to be your assistant on that Monday?"

He waved off the drink this time, the story was obviously coming to an end, and from the look of things, someone will have to drive Tim home.

"No, I was too terrified of the way I was feeling—that happened the next day. On the evening of Tuesday when I called her up and asked her about her day, she told me that she had lost her internship due to the company issued car that was found smashed up in the parking lot of the Dare guy's apartment when he was arrested. She sounded very sad and alone, so... the excellent idea popped into my head to offer her a job as my assistant till she could find something better. When I mustered enough courage to ask, she said yes and asked when she could start. I told her to come anytime she was ready (even though I knew how badly I needed an assistant). She chose the next day, so we met up at the company the next day."

"Cool Story Bro!" a now obviously drunk Tim said.

Andrew smiled and then finally asked, "What are you gonna do Jimmy?"

Jimmy stood up and looked down at his friend and said, "If you figure out the answer to that question before I do... Do me a favor and tell me, will you?"

PART 1—CUPID'S CURSE.

I was on a stage; the lighting was synonymous to that of a neighborhood with no transformer.

I laid on the stage bed blushing behind the covers in the throes of crowd jitters. I suddenly heard heavy footsteps approach the bed – the stagehand put on the sound effect that made it sound like a whole war band was gallivanting around my bedroom, public bedroom.

My cue to wake up!

I woke up to a similar scenario like the one I just dreamt – hearing familiar heavy footsteps approach as soon as I became aware.

It was Andrew, my photographer friend *slash* introverted roommate and his noisy feet I had to thank for all the racket...or maybe not.

Maybe it wasn't such a good idea to drink so much tequila after having just washed down a nice bowl of pepper soup with three bottles of Gulder, but that was last night's mistake.

I have decided recently, to ignore all decisions I make in the night since the trend has been I always regretted them, beat myself up about them and then go on to repeat them the next time the sky shooed the sun away and invited his cousin – the moon for a visit.

I heard him go through his usual routine of opening the blinds and then switching on the wall hung TV set, having experienced this torture so many times I knew the futility in trying to fake him out so I rolled over and squinted trying to ascertain what time it was. It looked like there was enough light in the room to fill *Thomas Edison's* workshop.

"Good afternoon, your Highness! And in case you were wondering. Today is weird-nesday." I heard the smug bastard say.

He was enjoying this. A part of me told me that this might actually be his favorite time of the day. If only denying him this pleasure could be motivation enough for me to get clean, but no, thinking about it even made me thirsty.

Of course, that barely audible voice of reason in my head couldn't keep his damn mouth shut, *'James, you are such a drunk' he said.* I could even see him in my mind's eye puffing on a pipe and shaking his oblong head disapprovingly – why he had a pipe I had no freaking idea, maybe I was still a little drunk.

PS; Guys! I have been told in the past that I have an overactive/wild imagination. What this means in the 'lay-est' of terms is that I see things that aren't there. (Advise; If you are like me, you may not want to ask your friend if he saw the humongous horns beneath the Maths teacher's scarf.)

I wanted to say something clever like "If your dad wasn't my boss I'd go all Dwayne Johnson on your ass right now" but all I could get out was this garbled rubbish *"eef loor daff vosint mny bosh ad glow dwade jonsttun on loor gasss vite noow"*

Damn Tequila.

I could hear him stifle a laugh as he audibly switched between channels. I knew the channel he was looking for and I had already put a parental lock on it the day before.

The guy with the pipe was grinning at this point.

I closed my eyes again to revel in my cleverness when suddenly I heard it. There was no mistaking it.

What could be so bad, you ask?

It was Indian music – pure, undiluted torture.

The bastard had outsmarted me again. I was baffled, how did he figure out the password? I opened my eyes slowly and painfully sat up ignoring the queasy way I was feeling just to see him on the floor in unfettered laughter.

"Dude, but why?" I asked him and managed to get it out properly this time "What did I do to deserve this, Andy?"

Take it from an experienced guy, the worst kind of hangover you can have is one in which you wake up to Indian music on full blast, I have Wemimo or Wendy as she liked to call herself to thank for that discovery, that wench loved her Indian soap operas.

He was finding it difficult to stop his laughing fits long enough to give me a reply. I just pursed my lips and fell back down onto the bed in resignation.

It was then I noticed the scrawled words on my palm. The words happened to have been written with a temporary marker. It spelled "Sevih".

Well, I thought, *that makes no sense,* but it was in my own writing. I tried to figure out what it could mean but thoughts slipped in my brain like a Canadian ice hockey player, so I gave it up and chalked it as drunken gibberish.

When he finally could speak, all he said was "BIGJUNK really, I thought you were kidding last night."

Dang it! I thought. Tequila-James must have said a little too much yesterday – I now recalled why I usually avoided drinking more than one shot of Tequila; Tequila-James was such a tattletale.

Thirty-minutes later I was seated at the dining space of our shared apartment trying to down a cup of gooey mush – a hangover cure I saw on the internet.

Apparently, it also made your penis grow larger and gave you a glow that made you irresistible to women. The dusty pack of condoms on the table before me though spoke volumes, not that I was the kind of guy that needed a concoction to attract women.

Damn, I needed to get laid, I thought to myself. Even Andrew was getting laid, technically banging your fiancée also counted even if it was only once a month when she visited.

Yeah, his fiancée worked in another geopolitical zone and she could only visit once every month.

I hated that b**tch. Andrew was never the fun guy I have come to lovingly detest around her, it's like there is a switch that she pulls when she lays her talons on him.

Anyway, back to the tale of my dry spell, Andrew had a hilarious notion that it had something to do with the last babe I dated – Paulina.

His theory was that she laid a curse on me to repel any girl that was not her. The funny eventuality was that things have gotten so bad that one very frustrating day I considered this crazy notion and tried to contact her – she had already gotten married and traveled out of the country.

Over the last few weeks, I've had experiences that could only be depicted with the phrase 'close but no cigar'.

A girl I met in the mall once gave me her cell no. I had been so impatient that I called her that very day, we met for a few drinks and made out a little, I was moving the party home and she was getting especially frisky when the police stopped us and asked us to get out of the vehicle. I was complying when I heard him mutter to his buddy in Yoruba that the babe in the vehicle was the one that gave him an STD.

I could hear little James crying behind the zipper, I took one look at the officer and deduced immediately that my passenger was a whore.

I settled both the officer and my companion and went home to console myself with vodka therapy – it never disappointed.

Why is not having sex for a few months so strange? I am guessing some of you are thinking it's a normal thing. Well, for a guy like me not having sex was a normal thing if eclipses happened every week or Good Ol' Nigeria became corruption free.

I am not a bragger and I value my wit way more than my appearance, but I seem to have what most ladies are looking for in their fantasy man – I had a perfectly fit body, I was not an inch below 6 ft., And a boring face, I had not.

It came in volumes – sex that is and I got used to it. Do I love having sex – who doesn't? I miss that feeling I get when little James makes a new friend.

Sounds of a muffled conversation came from the living room; Andy must be talking to 'you know who' over the phone.

I once caught him sexting – It was like Christmas came early, it was joke heaven for the next three days, the taunted became the taunter, but then he caught me jacking off and the tables turned.

I once bragged that rather than beat my meat, I'll just take a picture of my *junk* and put it up on eBay and sooner or later a hottie would show up for it. I suffered for that misstep for more than a month.

The true reason for my dry spell though was a very simple one – I was in *love*.

I remember the last time I was in *love*; I was in Junior secondary school at the time. Of course, it was no ordinary girl then as it is now – it was my English teacher. She was a Corper serving at my school at the time; she was so pretty she made English classes very interesting by just showing up.

I was in love with her or so I thought at that time, but I was beginning to rethink that notion.

The way I felt right now puts that other feeling I had in the past to shame. I was losing my mind and also my cool. I was losing everything gradually because I just couldn't man up to talk to the one girl that just might listen.

I even became a drunk.

You know what they say "You can take a man out of the bottle but you can never take the bottle out of the man" or was it "river" not "bottle". I don't have any idea if that quote works in this situation but I am using it.

Anyway, my phone buzzed in my pocket and I checked it to see it was a message from Toyin that triggered it. She usually texted before she entered the house ever since the day she walked in on me and one of my female companions.

She was not very pleased and I was distraught because I hadn't even been enjoying the sex that much –the other girl was basically raping me.

The message read *parking lot* – I guessed she would reach the apartment in about 10 minutes so I decided to get a little bit of fresh air.

I texted *Balcony* back to her and walked through the kitchen to the adjoining balcony. There were two lean back chairs on the balcony, I sat down, leaned back and heaved a huge sigh of relieve. The warm afternoon breeze seemed to do the trick of calming me – whenever she visited like this it was always very difficult to get a hold of myself.

The balcony was our spot of sorts, it had a wide view of the whole neighborhood. My building was basically the poorest on our line – ours was the first-storey building to be built in the locale, definitely not the last.

I suddenly recalled that the south stairwell was under repair and she will have to walk all the way to the east end of the building – that should delay her arrival even more.

So I settled into reminiscing as I waited, I remembered those nights when we would hang out on the balcony as we feasted on the view of suburban Ibadan and make up stories about what we thought was going on behind the neighbor's blinds in plain view.

I smelled her before I saw her, she smelled like freshly baked Shoprite bread and lemon. The former was because she lived opposite a bakery. I smiled and turned to greet her but froze when I saw she was in one of her moods.

She was blabbering animatedly into the phone's receiver as she approached the balcony and she was not smiling.

I didn't envy whoever was on the other end of that line – her insults ran through when she was pissed.

I turned back and faced my business as I began to regret that I didn't have a drink with me.

She sat down beside me and glanced at me as she cut off the call curtly.

"James, why do you look like you just came out of a car crash," she asked and she shifted the position of her chair so she was facing me.

".... aaah" I gasped, faking a very hoarse voice like that of a man that was dying of thirst.

"....aaah" I croaked yet again, I was smiling through all this though, "...need...a...drink."

She laughed, "That bad huh?" she asked.

I nodded vigorously with that ridiculous smile not leaving my face for once.

She laughed at that and went into the house and appeared a few minutes later with two bottles of beer.

I was not much of a beer person – I liked my drinks superhot, and she knew this so her choice of beer showed that she had a serious topic to discuss with me.

I accepted the beer when she handed it to me and took a gulp, then dramatically took a deep relieving breath "Sweetheart! You save my tainted soul once again" I said

She smiled as she replied me and said "Every soul deserves a second chance James ... yours merely needed a little elixir – which I provided"

"What price shall I pay my dame, sure a poor soul like mine must be lucky to have a guardian angel like you watching over me," I said with my flirtiest tone.

She just replied shrugging the flirt off by saying, "You sure don't pay me enough for all the work I do"

"Why do you say that babe?" I replied as I took another gulp from the drink, I still maintained my flirty tone.

Here it comes, I thought.

"Mr. James Olajide Davis do you know how much your drinking habit has cost you and your career..." she began, "Let me remind you of the shoot you ruined because you arrived late and drunk. How much people don't like you because you blow them off when they invite you for a drink and then you go on and drink yourself to stupor! How I literally had to beg to get the gigs I just got for you... I swear to God I deserve a damn medal!"

Well... I thought *that was a bit much than usual.*

"Sorry 'bout that," she said after a few breaths, "it's just that those wedding brats wanna kill me"

"Oh the wedding" I replied recalling that she had told me of a wedding she was meant to attend this month "...is that this weekend?"

"Yes... how many times do I have to tell you?" she replied somewhat miffed.

"Sorry, it's just that I have been a little forgetful lately," I said as I reached out my right hand and placed it on her shoulder apologetically.

"So... You know I won't be around for the next couple of days" she asked teasing me.

I put on my best crestfallen expression "Please don't leave me" I begged playfully.

"Well... you are in luck cause I got the venue you asked for" she replied, "so you can throw that party you've always wanted to throw – and by the way, this job was meant to be temporary for me remember?" she reached into her handbag and passed me a brochure she just extracted.

"The Novack's club joint?" I asked not believing "I didn't even know they accepted rentals – when I said venues I meant places like the hotel. How did you manage it?"

"Huh pfft...." She huffed, "I know a guy who knows a guy, it was nothing." She said waving it off and taking a gulp of the beer she had ignored up till this point.

"You truly are amazing..." I said with a very impressed look.

"I try..." she said

"Remember that you are gonna have to plan this whole thing for yourself...." She continued emphasizing that last word "...without me"

I looked thoughtful for a second then I said "First things first, borrow me your phone please"

I took the phone and called Andrew's fiancée's work no.,

I cleared my throat and did an impression of one of the most influential businessmen in the country silently to myself for practice. I smiled (I was gonna enjoy this).

I felt the line click and her voice came from the speakers; "Hello, Felicia Omisakin speaking." She said.

"Hello, this is Femi Jude Ali. Am I speaking with Felicia Aderonke Omisakin of Denga Incorporated?" I replied with my just rehearsed impression of the man.

"Ermm, Yes... Yes... it is. Um, you are speaking with her." A very flustered Felicia replied.

"Well, it has come to my attention that you are very efficient at your job at Denga and I just want you to know that you should keep up the good work. Now because of you, I get to hang out with Tade more often." I replied.

"Huh... thank you..." was all she could squeak out. One of the richest dudes in the country just complimented her; of course, she chooses this time to be speechless.

"Will you be free say 8:00 pm Saturday evening, I will like to meet and talk in person with Akintade's prodigy." I continued "He's spoken so highly of you, but I will like to witness this first hand."

"Yes, I'll be free sir" She breathed out, I could feel her trying to reign herself from jubilating.

"Well then, my assistant will contact you with the details, you have a nice day" and I hung up immediately with a wide grin on my face—obviously having fun.

I turned to see my assistant shaking her head with a disapproving smile, "When will you grow up and stop fucking with her?" she asks.

"When she leaves my boy alone?" I replied still smiling.

"Well good luck in your endeavors, I am taking my leave," she said "I need to quickly wrangle someone Asap"

She stood up to leave and as though on cue her phone began to ring loudly in my hand as it crooned the theme song of the Nigerian soap opera series; 'My Hero My LOVE" as written – a soap opera Toyin was addicted to.

Apparently, I thought to myself someone named Pam either had super powers or good timing as I handed her phone.

She glanced at the caller ID and hissed when she realized who it was as she cut off the call.

She leaned forward and planted a kiss on my forehead. I felt all intelligence excuse themselves from my brain for a split second – before they returned I already blurted; "Don't leave!" my voice sounded needy.

I suddenly realized what I had said and put the bottle in my mouth and gulped what was left of the beer.

She smiled and said, "Bye James" *She was the only one that still called me James.*

And then she was gone, wispy trails of a lemon-scented bakery trailing behind her.

***

I listened and a few minutes later I heard Andrew's cell ring in the living room. And as predicted he rushed over to my side to tell me the good news two minutes later.

"Felicia will not be coming home this weekend; she has a meeting with... wait a minute... My swatch says you can't guess who" he says.

I pretended like I didn't hear him the first time and said "What?"

"Felicia isn't coming this weekend because she is meeting a man of importance and I just bet my favorite watch that you can't guess the name of the person"

"Hmm..." I said as I raised a finger to my jaw as though I were trying to hazard a guess "... since you were stupid enough to tell me he was male the second time, that narrows it down... knowing you I know it's not her boss, you've met the boss more than a couple times and he considers you a son. So you wouldn't have that goofy-excited vibe I am detecting."

I smacked my lips as I stared at him as if I were really trying to put a puzzle piece together. I stopped and looked as if I wanted to give up.

Then I glanced at the watch and said "I just remembered a newspaper article I saw yesterday and guess who I saw on the front page... Mr. Akintade, Felicia's boss. So, I thought to myself –what was a picture Felicia's boss doing on the front page of the news? He sure wasn't that popular."

I paused for a minute. Looked at him square in the face and smiled, dropping the charade "He was beside that rich dude from the news, Mr. Femi Ali. Apparently, they were childhood friends." I stopped and now I was beaming at him "It's Femi Ali, isn't it?"

He smiled stiffly and forced a laugh. It was almost convincing but of course, I made the call so no luck for him.

"Wrong as usual, why am I not surprised ..." he said.

"Dude nice try," I say and I stretch my hand palms up and waited with that smile on my face. I knew how much he loved that watch.

His smile froze, then it was discarded a few seconds later, he then adapted the look of a pet owner that was about to give out his favorite pet.

"You caught me." He said "Just take care of it... till I can win it back from you. Knowing you, it shouldn't be that long."

I grinned wickedly at him and said "Considering what happened to my Rolex after you won it, I seriously doubt that"

"I'd rather smash it than place a bet with it or worse give you back directly" I continued.

He just shook his head, "That's unfair and you know it," he said, "Felicia took it without telling me, I told you a million times."

"Nah," I reply "She did it on purpose to spite me. She despises me. Trust me, I know."

He had a resigned look on his face like he was used to me saying things like that.

"My Gosh will you grow up already!" He said, he had that flare in the nose that usually signified he was either pissed or irritated "When will you give up this childish notion that the nicest girl on the planet is out to get you"

And there it was, the other Andy. I even had a secret nickname for him – 'Drew'.

"Yo! Calm down, dude... take it easy," I said as I raised my two arms in the form of innocence or surrender. "I was just saying" I added.

The looming fire in his eyes dimmed a little, but I could tell that he was not happy that his best friend and fiancée could not reconcile their differences. I knew he blamed me mostly for this. Finally, when I was sure 'Drew' was not in control anymore, I said "G-Andy, get off your high horse. I need your help."

He must have heard the seriousness in my tone because he paused and really looked at me for a moment. "Really, finally decided to go to the witch doctor I recommended?" He said with a mocking grin – dang he stole that grin right out of my handbook. Well, that's as much prove I needed that my friend has forgotten whatever got him riled up a few mins ago.

So cocky as ever but seriously, he asked "How can I help you this day, Maestro Jimmy"

"Well, since your girl won't be coming this weekend, we are gonna throw a party," I said still maintaining seriousness.

He smiled and I knew he was down "Let's throw a freaking party!" He said.

PART 2—ENEMIES ARISING

I laid on my bed two days later, I stared at the ceiling and gulped. My liquor guy was not picking my calls. That asshole was gonna get me in trouble with 'Drew'.

After agreeing to plan everything with him, I had been avoiding him. I did forward a link to him though.

Yeah, guilty as charged – I googled party planning. I sent him the 'Wikihow' link on planning parties that popped up and put my phone straight into airplane mode.

Now you are thinking, don't you guys live together? How do you avoid someone you live with?

Well, I took a modeling Gig that Toyin got for me before she left –that took the whole of my Thursday and I drank well... into the midnight, only stopping by the house a couple times.

That's how you do it.

Have I really fallen so low so fast? I mused. Now I just was an all-out drunk, *captain jack sparrowing* my way through life.

The cunning bastard took a hint and wrote a hilarious note on the fridge door that said; he was not pissed and that I should just take care of providing the liquor that he was going to handle the other things.

I tried Aliyu's number for the umpteenth time and then gave up. *This was just great* – I thought.

I tried to guess why the guy that normally picked after first ring every time was not picking my call. I knew it had to be intentional so I decided to pay him a visit.

I got to his usual place of hunting around 5 pm in the evening. I knew I was cutting it close, but I had to wait till I was sure he was going to be there. I snuck in the back so that if he saw me approaching he couldn't skedaddle.

The place was a bar, though not a very prominent one I used to hang out here as an undergraduate a few years back. This was how I met Aliyu, he was a very large and lousy man, though strangely he quieted once you got enough liquor in him.

Though from the look of things and from the booming cement-timbered voice I heard as soon as I entered the bar I knew Aliyu was not inebriated in any way.

He was having a conversation with his brother – who owned the bar by the way. He was laughing hysterically when I got to where the conversation was taking place at the far end of the bar. I didn't even need to walk silently, his voice masked my approach.

I cleared my throat and I pulled out an old nickname "Aliyu, oko Aliya" I said.

The way he froze when he heard my voice behind him, I knew something was really wrong. A very red-faced Aliyu turned around to regard me, his expression was a hybrid mixture of disgust, rage and contempt with flakes of disappointment sprinkled on top.

I just stared, 'words' in my mouth couldn't find 'air' in my lungs.

He flicked his gaze at his brother and when he spoke his voice was scarily low and laced with so much venom it poisoned the air with an even stranger vibe – violence. "Shina, I thought I told you to stop this 'scum' from entering this establishment."

Shina was not a very expressive man, he was blunt and also a very hard read. So, it was very difficult for me to actually tell if he was kidding when he said "I just thought you were drunk rambling Ali. I mean its Smiling Jimmy we're talking about here."

"Smiling Jimmy is dead to me," he replied his brother, with the same expression hanging on his face – if possible it even got scarier.

He was visibly squeezing his knuckles like he was fighting an urge and with that little gesture, I took a step backwards.

I knew there was no way to break through the three-inch titanium wall that was his resolve to very visibly shun me. So, I did the next best thing.

I turned to face Shifu – this was the nickname we gave Shina because he behaved like the Chinese monk martial arts teachers we saw in movies.

"Please Shifu, do you have any idea why Ali is so mad?" I asked calmly.

This seemed to set Ali off though, and he tensed like a panther that was about to pounce, but before he made a step, Shifu placed his palm on his shoulder—a gesture for him to stay put.

Shifu was a guy you did not want to cross, he was a black belt in bar-fighting—yea, he did not earn his name from his behavior alone. He knew how to have a conversation with his fists. Having seen him fight a couple times a part of me believed he relished the rare thrill of pummeling other people – with good cause.

"I will have no fight in my bar today, Aliyu." he said flatly.

Visibly, the tinge of violence that shrouded his irises faded away and he just deflated.

"This is about that girl Pamela girl, isn't it?" Shina continued. If I was not mistaken, I detected a hint of amusement this time around.

"THAT! THAT! ASSHOLE SLEPT WITH MY GIRL." He bellowed "He called her up and then fucked her senseless," He said more quietly this time, though the bar was basically empty except for the obviously beer-chugged individual in the middle booth.

I was so stunned I had the same expression we all tried to mimic as kids when we were accused of stealing meat from the pot – mine was the real deal though. And of course, my next words came out in auto-pilot.

"Girl...? Sleep...? Me...?" I stuttered – Sound familiar.

My right hand was on my chest like one of those rare occasions that I decided to recite the national pledge properly in secondary school. I was so tired; the ridiculousness of the situation threw me into hysterics.

Now it was Ali's turn to look confused.

"Do you not like all your teeth intact?" He asked, regaining some of his almost obsolete Bruce lee spirit.

He really looked so pathetic that I even tried to recall any girl in my past that I slept with that had the name, Pamela.

I was busy racking my brain with a weird smile on my face that won't go away when I heard Shifu ask his second surgically placed question of the evening,

"When did this occur?" He asked

"Last week!" Ali said still fuming

I sighed slightly out of relieve when I heard him say that.

"Oh!" I breathed "In that case, you really are mistaken, Aliyu."

I looked to his brother for a little support, what I saw there, in the beige canvas that was his face seemed sympathetic or sad – with Shifu you really couldn't be sure.

I admit I was 'that guy'.

That guy that was reputed to... you know have more game than other guys.

Granted, I was that guy that his weekly bed tally usually had more numbers than the amount of beer bottles my lightweight friend Andy could stomach in one night. But that dude had been dead for a while now.

That dude was news and like every other gossip worthy celebrity's personal life experience, it soon became public knowledge.

He leaned forward and whispered something to Ali and I saw the way his facial expression transitioned from; incredulity to amusement to thoughtfulness and finally unadulterated rage. Luckily, this time though, it was clear his rage was not directed at me.

He just yammered a couple of insulting phrases in his home tongue then he turned to me and he began to apologize.

"James you have to forgive me," he said "Shifu just told me about your se... eh err Condition and I truly feel bad for rubbing salt in your wound."

My God this was embarrassing. Smile gone, I said as I made up my mind to get the hell out of the bar, "Goodbye Aliyu. Shifu, thanks for the save"

Shifu just nodded and lifted his hand from Ali's shoulder.

"If you ever need anything, just call me," Aliyu said.

I was almost at the door when it hit me, I still hadn't gotten the drinks.

"You know what, maybe there is something you can do?" I said as I turned around to face him.

When I left that bar I was beaming, obviously, way chipper than I should have been at that moment, but to the gallows with my pride. Aliyu just agreed to supply all the liquor for the party for free.

Later that night, as I snacked on my happy hour stash of peanuts, and was about to forward the location of the party to Aliyu, I stumbled upon an old unread message that drew my attention.

I opened it and read it, it was a short message. Apparently, she—the unknown person, was out to get me, she wrote and I quote "You ruined my twin sister's life, so I am going to destroy yours." A sentence she then ended with a ludicrous amount of Emojis (not the nice ones).

I stopped chewing the peanuts, something about the note making me lose my appetite and my chirpy mood all together.

Sheesh, What the hell! My life was looking like an episode of a Telemundo soap opera. I mean, what's with all the bad luck and a vendetta.

I closed my eye, and took a deep breath and strangely like a superhero movie a memory came unbidden to me;

It was the finale of a three-day revival my local childhood church was hosting and the preacher man was preaching about the arrows that were fired from one's origins or home village that prevented one's advancement. Twelve-year-old Jimmy in this memory was seated in the back trying to get Funmi, a girl he just broke up with, from putting her hand up his boxers.

The preacher then asked the whole congregation to rise up and say this prayer. Since he said all this in undiluted Yoruba, I will try to translate this as well as I can.

The prayer point goes "There are those that their destiny has been compromised. The meaning of their life stolen from under their noses by some Dracula-looking mother freaking 21st-century witches. They needed no inspiration all they wanted was blood. Scream Blood! Blood! 5x. Scream Blood of Jesus! Say, Jesus, I am here with you tonight *to something..." That's about all I could remember.*

The most vivid part of that night's memory though was the way that the Girl that was just trying to touch my privates a few seconds before, began to scream 'blood!' beside me. The way she looked like a fiery dragon under the filament bulb scared me senseless.

Goosebumps appeared on my skin as that memory flashed through my head. The memory of that girl that night had become the apparition that represented Pamela in my brains now.

I yawned twice, fear was driving whatever vitality I had left away.

Poof! Off I went like a light bulb.

***

The figure named 'Nightmare' who was lurking in the corner all this while on its lonesome, just smirked and walked in to do its job.

PART 3—THE PARTY

I woke to the smell of night terrors.

My knuckles were sore from gripping the sweat-soaked sheets too tightly during the night.

I consulted my thalamus or wherever the hell we store memories in our brain and I crossed out 'woke up sweaty from nightmares' with dripples of a tippex invented by the Russians – Vodka.

With immaculate lettering that will make even Michel de Angelo jealous, I replaced it with 'Got in a fight', that felt too vague so I added 'with Ali and his brother'.

Of course, the sarcastic dude with the pipe decided to speak up this time "Why not just add *'and won'* while you are at it?". He was dressed strangely like Rowan Atkinson's Character – Mr. Bean. So ironically, I threw him into a mental pot and sealed the lid.

The party was this evening, so I was free until then. I decided to check the sports channel for news on the football matches that were to hold today. Ooh, I exclaimed. Chelsea was going to be playing Arsenal, what a nice coincidence.

> *"The author says before he brings in the next character, he wants you guys to know that the*

character is way crazier than is portrayed, the version of his character portrayed in this tale has been heavily redacted and as you will all see for yourselves - with good cause as well."

Time to call Tiny Tim. Tim was the single craziest and the most honest guy, I have ever met in my life. I ran into him at one of his Mistresses husband's housewarming party, he was looking for anybody with a spare condom, I happened to have a spare so I gave it to him.

After the party, he came to thank me and ask me where I got such good quality rubber and we hit it off from there. Ever since then I have seen him do things that only happened in Adam Sandler's Movies.

He once had sex with all the females in an entire family in a single day; starting from the mother to her twin daughters and they all knew about it.

Now this next one you might not believe.

We were once caught in a bank robbery situation and tiny Tim wanted to pee. My very good friend walks up to the scariest of the masked gun-wielding assailants and asked for permission to use the toilet.

The funny thing was that they let him. They even shared a joke.

By the time the armed robbers were leaving the bank, he was on first name basis with their leader and he was flirting with the female amongst them.

He single-handedly slept with an entire modeling agency one month because he was bored and I quote 'the weather was too dry'.

"Hey, Author dude!
You were right, they
really don't believe me.
They think my stories
are embellished."

His one true virtue, however, was that he was very honest, he never lied to the women he had coitus with. Also, he was the only person in my circle with more nicknames than I did.

Also, I feel it's important to mention that he was in no way good looking, neither was he of tall or medium height.

He looked like a dwarf and the smurf had a lovechild. But he had this rough look about him that the ladies loved plus his eyes were an uncharacteristic Hazel.

His phone rang and after like two rings I heard his voice from the receiver.

"Smiling Jimmy! How the f**k are you this morning?" He said, "Can I ... Can I call you back, I am kinda in the middle of something now?" And I felt the line go dead.

Well, there goes the idea of watching a soccer match with a perverted psychopath.

So I laid back on the bed and picked up my phone to see a news notification, the headlines said that Femi Jude Ali was out of the country to have some talk with another rich dude from Dubai.

That didn't seem right so I checked it again carefully and I noticed that I read that wrong, it said: "Femi Jude Ali divorces his wife."

What a surprising turn of events, Femi Ali was divorcing his wife.

Okay, I needed a drink. I grabbed my shorts and I made my way to my makeshift bar in the living room.

I saw another note from Andrew on the fridge door as I went to retrieve ice to chill my drink. It said; he was out preparing the venue and I should not drink too much sparkling water. Apparently, he had replaced all the Vodka in my bar with water –his justification being that I covered my end of the deal poorly because of the late arrival of the drinks.

I hoped to God that he didn't touch my special stash.

Sadly, I wondered what he would have done if no drink had arrived or worse if he found out about the prank I played on his wife to be.

I dozed off on the couch a few minutes later and woke up three hours later.

I checked my phone and saw that I had couple missed calls from an unknown number.

My phone lit up, Tiny Tim was calling.

I picked up the phone briskly and said "Tiny Devil!"

He replied like he always did "Smiling Jimmy, F**k I missed you." He said, "Where you at?" He asked.

"At home..." I began to say but he cut me off.

"You mean that apartment that you refused to equip with toilet rolls." And I heard a toilet flush from the phone receiver.

The sound of the toilet flushing sounded a lot louder than it should.

Wait a minute, I thought.

I covered the phone's receiver, but I could still hear the toilet. "Hey! Are you in my apartment?" I asked.

"Nah, I just walked into your neighbor's apartment and used their toilet." He replied, "But the real question here though is what are you doing on their couch?"

"Tiny Tim; one. Smiling Jimmy; zero."
I replied as I cut off the call. I locked my
phone screen and I checked my face for any
new additions.

I recalled the last time I slept off
around Tim, I woke with a very graphic
image of a phallus on my face.

A few seconds later, I felt rather than
saw him behind me, I was still busy checking
if I woke up the same way I slept with no
Tim additions.

"When did you get here?" I asked
finally when I was done checking as well as I
possibly could without looking stupid.

"About two hours ago," he said, "by the
way, there are three very gorgeous girls in
your room freshening up, I hope you don't
mind."

"Damn it! Tim, the last girls you
brought here stole my grandfather's watch."
I said.

"Oh! Wait a minute, about that..." he
said as he started patting his pockets looking
for something ".... there you are," he said as
his face lit up and he dug his hands into his
back pocket and brought out my
grandfather's watch.

Even though I was still pissed about
the girls, I was genuinely glad to see the
watch again. I reached out my hand to collect
it, then thought better of it.

"Did you wash those hands of yours?" I asked, shifting back and feigning disgust.

"Well… Since you don't seem to want it back…" he made a beeline for the trash can but I interrupted him mid-step and snatched the watch from him.

He just laughed at me and went into my room to get the girls. When they came out I was shocked to see one of those girls he brought over the last time. He never brought any girl back here, it was like one of his unwritten rules.

Whilst the girls chatted amongst themselves, he came over and was like "Sorry bro, I asked them if you could pitch into our activities tonight and they said no."

I was checking the girls out when the strangest thing happened. The duo I didn't recognize began to make out with each other. I was stunned, but neither my friend nor the other girl batted an eyelash. This was normal. "Wait a minute, are they gay?" I asked innocently curious.

"Yea, I met them on Snap Chat. They wanted the male experience and they said that a friend of theirs recommended me." He replied not taking his eye off them for a second.

"What about the other girl, what's her story?" I asked.

He just gave me an offhanded reply "Long story! Let's just say she's special."

He said that last word loud enough for her to hear and he beckoned the girls over. He walked up to meet them and he went in between the lesbian girls, who he happened to be taller than by the way and placed his arm across their shoulders.

They all made their way towards the apartment door.

"See you during the party dude. I and these ladies have some unfinished business," he said out loud without looking back.

When he was just outside the apartment door, he turned around with a mischievous grin on his face "And by the way, the landlord said I should tell you that he has removed the barricade on the stairs but that it should still be used with care" he said and with that, he was gone.

***

The party had already started by the time I got there. I was the soberest I had been in the last few months. I was tired and I knew something really wasn't right as I scanned the terrain and tried to get the whole sense of the party.

By *'sense of the party'*, let me educate those of you that do not know; there are three kinds of parties.

We have the gay parties and these generally describe parties where the male population dominate with about 70%.

Next is the normal *slash* balanced party and in these kinds of parties, girl populations dominate with about 51% to 55%.

Last but not least my favorite, the Lez. Party, basically in this kind of party we have about 80% population of the party being female.

From the looks of this one though, I really shouldn't have kept my hopes up. I mean, I knew the kind of person Andrew was and I still let him send the invitations.

There were so many guys in here that I couldn't even see any women in my peripheral.

As I glanced around, I saw a very pretty lady by the side all alone. I checked out myself in general and saw that I looked amazing. I put on my most charming smile and approached.

I felt my phone vibrate in my pocket but decided to ignore it. Everybody else vanished but the pretty lady, for the next few minutes all I wanted to see was her.

My phone was still vibrating in my pockets when I got to where she was sitting.

She was really pretty up close and she looked familiar.

I ignored the ringing phone and said: "Hey there pretty lady, I need help figuring out what I just wandered into." Of course, my most charming smile was elegantly plastered upon my façade.

She looked puzzled. *Perfect* I thought.

"Pardon my forwardness. I'm James, Jimmy for short. I was just wondering what kind of ar-MAN-geddon, I just walked into." I said.

She chuckled. It was a sweet sound – like peanut butter with peanut lumps. I nearly lost my courage, but I smiled my doubts off.

"Ar-man-geddon, I like that," she replied with the most dazzling smile I have ever seen in my life. "I am Pam, Pamela for short." She said all this with a perfect British accent.

Damn it. My phone was ringing again. "I'm sorry Pamela. I'll be right back." I said and I excused myself from her side.

I checked the phone to see it was Andrew. "Hey! Where have you been? I've been looking for you all over." I shouted into the mouthpiece of the phone and pressed the device tightly to my ear so that I could hear over the ambient music.

"Where have you been? Because I am very sure you are not at the same party as I am," he replied. "Listen to the music in the background"

I covered my other ear and listened carefully. I could hear it, but barely.

"Oh, is that "Teach me how to Dougie" by Cali swag playing over the speakers?" I asked.

"Yes, so where the heck have you been since morning?" He bellowed back.

"Where you told me to meet you, Club 3B!" I replied, starting to get pissed.

"I wrote it on the fridge door that it was Club 4B, directly above the Gay club 3B," He said, then I felt the realization hit him "Oh shit! You are in the Gay club! Hehe! That's definitely going in my diary." He said with booming laughter.

He started to say something, but I cut him off and checked behind me for the woman I was just talking to – She was gone.

Too bad. I had a feeling I would like her.

By the time I got to the actual party I was pissed. Very pissed at Andrew but as soon as I entered I changed my mind.

Remember my little lecture about types of parties, I had just walked into my favorite.

Yea, you guessed it, a lez party. It stunned me speechless.

How did Andrew do this? I thought to myself. The first person to spot me though was Tiny Tim. He approached and said, "Where is that roommate of yours?"

He grabbed me suddenly and kissed me on the forehead "let me give you a kiss, do pass it on whenever you see him. "Tell him it's from me."

Then he sauntered off to make mischief somewhere else.

I walked further into the party looking for Andy when I spotted him having a discussion with the DJ about something.

I approached, all the annoyance I had for him just moments ago had evaporated.

"You really outdid yourself here Mr. Smandy Pants," I said as soon as I got within earshot of him.

He turned and watched me approach, and said loud enough for me to hear the DJ "...and that is the man whose excellent idea this all is... just showing up for his own party," he said glancing at watch like a boss that had been expecting an employee and just saw him arrive.

Then again lower this time "He was busy with the men upstairs"

From the expression of the DJ, it was clear that he knew that there was a gay club upstairs.

"Truly, what I saw in the kitchen was that the party was gonna hold at 3B" "I remember cause it was scrawled in that your ridiculous handwriting with a red pen.

"Ha-ha, very funny, pretend as if you really read the note properly," he said, "well you guessed wrong cause I wrote my note with a blue pen."

"No, really. The note I saw was, written in red. Even the one you left today"

He looked like he was about to say something, but something or someone distracted him momentarily.

I turned around to check what all the hassle was about and I shocked to see a chick I never expected to see tonight, her countenance dwarfed that of the other girls around and she was looking so fucking dope my jaws were almost lying flat.

I turned to see she was having a similar effect on my roommate. She was coming towards us and considering the glowing gleam coming from Andy, I inferred that he too saw what I saw.

When she spoke her voice sounded like the sweetest thing – like honey wrapped in peanut butter with peanut lumps. (Obviously I love peanuts!)

"How are you doing, Andy?" She said when she got within earshot.

"Hi, Toyin?" He replied.

Hell no I thought. Romance between this two? I'll kill myself!

I stretched my hand forward and offered her a handshake and said charmingly "I don't believe we've been introduced Toyin, I'm Jimmy"

She smiled at my joke and went along with it "Oh, I know very well who you are Mr, James" she said.

"Oh..." I said not looking surprised ".... I see Andrew here had a lot to say about me didn't he?"

I looked at him with a slightly menacing smile.

But she snipingly replied, managing an exact replica of my smile "No, he said nothing. You are a popular young man."

"It was Toyin that assisted me to make the party this cool," Andrew said.

Figures, I thought.

"Well, nice to meet you then," I said,

I gestured her over to the side and said more seriously "What a pleasant surprise.... I thought you will be three feet deep in shades of white by now."

The music suddenly pitched upwards and got so loud that it drowned the voices of the people around us.

She leaned closer to my ear so that I could hear her very clearly and said: "I came back a few hours ago, the bride finally succeeded in pissing me off so much that I had to leave."

"But you don't come across as someone who gets as angry as that." I said, "What happened?"

"Well, seems you've never witnessed a bride before her wedding day. They tend to be bitches –and this my friend is no ordinary bride," she said, "Annoying people is her hobby!"

"Then, my lady will you please stay with me through the night as I face this weird thing I created," I said as I grabbed her arm.

"No, I can barely walk as it is..." she said "I am taking my leave... this night you have to dance to the beat of your own music." She smiled at that line.

She slithered out of my fingers and like a breath she was gone. I suddenly began to crave a drink very badly.

I scanned around and located a sizeable amount a few feet away. I was halfway there when my phone began to vibrate again.

A special track; *witch of the west*, was playing in the club so I had an inkling as to who it was and not surprisingly, it was Felicia.

I didn't even think, I picked the call to gloat.

However, instead of a beat down and sad Felicia answering the phone, she sounded rather upbeat.

"Hey, Jimmy.... You there? ...I called to say thanks..." she began, "your little prank worked wonders for me. Turns out Mr. Femi Ali just fired his assistant so he answered the phone himself when I called, and guess what? I just had dinner with him."

She paused "So thank you again and check your inbox will you?" She said and then cut the call off.

Now I really needed a drink, so I fastened my pace towards the liquor while I brought out my phone and opened up my inbox and there, written in all capital letters was 'must read'.

I opened the email to see a message about an HIV Campaign, and an image.

Funny though, I thought *I have not yet started to take alcohol (*though I had arrived at the table) *and I was already seeing things.*

I saw a picture of me in the epicenter of the poster surrounded by a couple presumed HIV patients.

The Jimmy in the poster had a huge smile plastered on his face – the same smile that earned me my nickname.

It really was a picture of me, I realized –and I looked like one of the patients.

Hell no! I thought.

My full name was even written on the poster. But I did not recall taking that particular picture.

Then I noticed the combination of clothing and it jolted my memory and I remembered clearly that day I had gone to a shoot drunk.

So drunk that I didn't know what the shoot was about, Tim and Andrew had picked me up later and told me that they had to beg them to not publicize.

I really hit rock bottom that time – they had banned me from alcohol for a while after that.

I quickly put two and two together, but no further thoughts were processed at that moment.

The gears in my head ground and clinked from overuse and then suddenly clicked back into place as thought processing began again.

The poster was the reason for my dry spell.

I have got the *hives*! – hives represents a situation that everybody around you thinks that you are HIV positive.

Now carefully thinking about it, I must have realized it on Tuesday night while I was drunk and scrawled it on my palm but for some reason unknown I must have scrawled it backward as "Sevih".

Who else knew about this? I asked myself. Andy? Tim? Toyin…?

As soon as the full extent of my situation hit, I became very self-aware, I grabbed a bottle of liquor and headed in the presumed direction of the back exit.

I saw Andy and redirected my course.

He saw me coming and took in the expression on my face and apprehension flashed before his face – the look of a guilty man.

When I was close enough to him that he couldn't easily slip away "Well... well... young man! YOU'VE GOT SOME EXPLAINING TO DO!" I bellowed.

He moved backwards – I don't think I had ever been so pissed before in my life.

"Hold on... I can explain" he said

"Really..." I said incredulously "you can explain?"

"Yea... Seeing as all this was your fault to begin with... that is all I can do!"

We were basically drawing a lot of attention as we yelled at each other.

So I said a little calmer this time "Okay... I am listening."

"Well... Toyin called us that you showed up for the shoot Drunk and told us to go get you... remember she was not around. Tim picked me up and we showed up at the venue of the shoot and asked for the guy in charge. They took us to see him and there you were on the monitor in front of him... they had taken a couple of shots."

"Yeaaa..." I said scratching my head "I vaguely recall taking pictures... but I thought it was drunken imagination."

"Noooo Dude... turns out you arrived for the shoot early and were strangely cooperative but obviously drunk... The director didn't want to reschedule so he took a couple shots with an improvised concept and they seemed to like it... so much that he was gonna pay extra for the shots."

"Wait a minute... and you guys let them?"

"Well, we weren't going to... but Toyin called and said that the director spoke to her and that we should just get you out of there – we didn't even know what the hell the shoot was about. So we left with you... and that was that, until a few days later when I saw the poster..."

"Damn it! Why didn't you say anything?" I asked.

"Well, Toyin said she had told them to get rid of it... or something like that, but I and Tim kinda had a silent agreement to keep our mouths shut and let your crush break the bad news... I actually thought she already did when you began to drink again... but I figured she hadn't a few days ago and I told you. Tuesday night I think?"

"Yea... when I was conveniently drunk!" I said.

"When are you ever sober!" he snapped back, "At least I tried to tell you... I can't say much about that pretty assistant of yours!"

"You know what, I am sure she had her reasons... The truth is that either you or that tiny devil could have broken the news but you had to let that... that fiancée of yours do it..."

"Oh grow up James... she had her reasons?" he said.

"I'm sure she did!" I replied more defensively.

"Oh, just like Felicia had a reason for telling you?"

I stared at him stunned—he knew!

"Yea... she told me—why do you think I got rid of your liquor. That was payback for Wednesday."

"You know what... I can't stand seeing you right now" I said and I stormed away.

I made my way towards the backroom again.

When I got there I saw a door. I gave it a little shove to see that it was open. It led into a room lit with nothing but moonlight and the faint luminescence from the club behind me.

Illuminated in the little glow was a bench, I approached still deep in melancholy and only noticed the figure on the bench when I moved closer.

"Hey there..." I said by way of greeting—startled.

"The figure faced away from the dim light. But upon hearing my greeting, the figure turned around and I saw a smile I just saw a few mins ago.

"Pamela...?" I asked

"Yes, it is me." She replied and she gestured for me to sit down opposite her.

I complied. "What a nice way to bump into you again, I thought I'd never see you again," I said then I paused, and really looked at her catching her eye.

"What were you doing in the gay bar, if you don't mind my asking," I asked as coolly as I could muster.

She smiled again and drawled sultrily with that elegant British accent of hers "I could say the same to you."

"Oh for me it was just a simple sprinkle of illiteracy in my friend and roommate," I said playfully, "what about you?"

"Well..." she said measuring her words carefully "I guess one could say the same for me as well though in my case it was my sister and hers was just plain carelessness."

"I assume you are the one they call smiling Jimmy?" She asked.

"Yea, something like that," I said with a sheepish smile.

"You seem very calm –maybe you can help," I said taking in her general mood.

She raised her eyebrows at me.

I began to dwell on what brought me to the backroom again and said, "It's like I am in a wedding and the preacher says 'Jimmy's face... are you willing to take 'Brick Wall' as your lawfully wedded wife till death do you part?" There I am in the front of the church, suddenly it dawns on me that it was a question so I could say no. I opened my mouth to say 'no thank you' but instead what comes out is YES!"

I suddenly got into character "...I try to run but I am rooted to spot as my 'bride' rushes in for a kiss. Our kiss was literal fireworks –debris flew everywhere. Funny thing was, the more she kissed me over the last few months the duller the pain got, up until now...."

I paused, inhaled loudly and shook my head slightly.

"...now I and the wall have come to terms. I do not tense before I kiss her anymore I just smile – a widening of lips much like that of a stitched up scare crow's lips."

The temperature of the room was cool and the dank quietness of everything suddenly made it all look eerie, that and the moonlight filtering in from its sole window.

"Funny you should say that; I saw a huge red brick wandering around the party. She was looking for her husband?" She said barely hiding a smile as she said this.

I suddenly ducked and looked like a tenant that was trying to avoid his landlord because of overdue rent. "Damn it!" I said tersely "... that bitch followed me here!"

"How do you stay passive when life throws a *trailer of shit* at you?" I asked again seriously sitting up properly.

"I was just about to ask you the same exact question," she said faking a surprised look.

That piqued my interest "Really?" I said.

"Yea, I know what you speak of." She replied after a short breath, "When life throws a turd at you; you simply become a toilet – it's that simple." I almost didn't get what she was saying because of her accent.

"Well, young lady..." I said with a perverted smile "every public toilet has a male and female section."

"Is there a question in there somewhere?" she asked, playing along with my ridiculous line of thought.

She reached into her purse and brought out a stick of cigarette and a lighter. She took my hand and put the cigarette in it. I raised it to my lips as if in a trance.

"I guess my question is more of an offer," I said.

"And..." she said.

She ignited the lighter and held it before her eyes, the light sparkled in her eye and just for a moment, I thought she was Toyin.

"Will you be the female toilet to my male toilet?" I breathed just imagining for a moment she was Toyin.

She lit the cigar in my lips. I took a long drag and exhaled smoothly.

The exercise seemed to calm me down. I am no smoker, but I indulged in the occasional smoke, how she had guessed that, I didn't know.

I removed the cigarette gently from my lips and I passed it to her. She made no effort to collect it from my hand.

Her expression indicated that she wanted me to put it in her lips myself, I didn't want to read into this little gesture, but I complied – a little too much though.

I took another drag, and I was rewarded with an impish raised eyebrow from her which I ignored as I grabbed and kissed her – sharing the smoke with her. She seemed shocked by my forwardness but didn't object to the kiss. She kissed me back harder.

I know what you are thinking, what about Toyin?

Well, at that moment I was not thinking about the future, all I thought about was the amount of the british I could suck from her lips.

The guy with the pipe showed up in my peripheral vision. He was playing the bagpipe and tap dancing. When he noticed the attention, he winked at me.

I wondered how it would seem to anyone that happened to stumble upon this sight.

The vigor with which she kissed like she wanted to pass a message. Her hands began to roam my body.

Her right palm tried a pickup line with Little Jimmy.

Little Jimmy perked up and suddenly began paying rapt and hard attention.

Buttons popped as my fingers found courage—a little more than courage of course.

Her right palm and Little Jimmy had hit things off and were already making out at this point.

Finally, I thought, the dry spell was over!

I knew something was wrong when the mental image of the guy with pipe vanished into smoke.

My phone began to vibrate and she jumped—startled, putting a stop to our activities. I grabbed the phone furiously and switched it off as I felt the sexual tension ebb.

I thought too soon and jinxed it.

A few minutes later back to our previous dressed states, we shared a shot of the rum I had brought along with me.

"Fuck!" I said after I passed the bottle to her.

"I truly cannot know how you must be feeling about the poster..." she said as she caught her breath finally. She seemed amused.

I froze and almost choked on the drink as I was taking a swig from the bottle directly. I sputtered out "You know about that?"

She stood and regarded me as though she were just seeing me. "Of course, I know about it silly, I planned it."

I heard what she said but in the milliseconds it took for my brain to process, I could have sworn that time slowed down like in the movies.

Slow James watched as not so slow Pamela brought up a very fast right hook and promptly introduced it to his unsuspecting face.

For the second time in this tale 'off I went like a light bulb'.

***

Lust stared at its buddy Hallucination as it paced. It was waiting for a fellow figure who should have been here by now.

'Shit, where the hell is 'nightmare' at?' said its friend out loud '... She knocked him out ahead of schedule.'

76

'Oh shit! They are moving him already.' Hallucination squeaked as It began to move towards the unconscious figure *'I better jump in there before it's too late.'*

***

I woke up tied up to a tree.

It looked to be nowhere in particular that I could pick out of memory.

It took a while for the defective processor in my skull to boot.

I felt like I had been hit in the face with a bat... hit in the face so hard I passed out... I slowly deduced. After which my attacker whoever it was then brought me to wherever the hell I am now.

"Pamela!" I said out loud and I heard muffled laughter from behind the tree I was tied to.

"Figure it out yet?" Asked Pamela. "Still booting....? Let me jog your memory."

Suddenly I felt a hand reach over from behind the tree and rest gently on the center of my head and for the second time in the last two days, I recalled that day, the day of the finale of the revival in my childhood church though this time I could see it more in detail.

Then it clicked and I recalled where I knew her from.

Turns out I didn't put up much of a fight to the girl that was making advances to me that day as I may have portrayed previously.

In fact, it was never her that I saw illuminated in the bulb light, it was Nike.

I had just broken up with the girl that was fondling my nether regions to date Nike – who happened to be the prettiest girl in our little local town then.

It wasn't news that everybody that knew her was amazed by her beauty, but there was talk in town about her being a little bonkers.

It was whispered slightly that one day she attacked her then-boyfriend with a set of scissors for no apparent reason.

No one knew this for sure but 12-year-old version of me gave no credence to the rumors.

Well, until that moment when I noticed her shouting along with the ambient congregation.

"Blood!" She screamed staring right at me with insanity dancing in the two tiny orbs that occupied her eye holes.

She had scared me so much that I broke things off with the other girl immediately. I waited a week, then I dumped her as well. Three months later, I moved.

Another unbidden memory flashed before me.

I was still twelve in this memory, we had just moved into a new apartment and was watching the news because we had not set-up the antenna and there were no other stations on, when I saw a clip of a familiar building burning. It was the building we had just moved out of. I couldn't shake a weird feeling that something was off, but I soon forgot about that little irritating feeling that something was not quite right.

Somehow at that moment, tied to that tree I suddenly knew without a doubt that it was Nike that was behind it.

I could see a vague memory of her stalking me for weeks, then another of her talking to the new tenant when she chalked up enough courage to stop stalking me and approach, being told that I had moved, and finally of her lighting the keg of Gasoline she saw while storming out of the building.

I felt the hand lift and I suddenly felt weaker than I was a few seconds and also queasy. "What did you do to me?" I gurgled.

My head was hanging low at that point and I was so weak that it was the rope that was holding me upright.

"Just a little, mind-melding exercise to open your eyes." She said with a perfect replica of Cecilia's voice as she walked from the back of the tree into view. She still looked beautiful as ever and I could barely stand to look at her now that I knew – people had died in the fire that happened that day.

"Why go through all that trouble...?" I asked too weak to play any more games "what did I do to deserve all this?"

She laughed, I recalled that laughter very well – having heard it so many times over the phone when I was talking to my Assistant.

The guy with the pipe appeared again, this time though he looked strangely like one of the pictures of Einstein in his white lab coat. He was tapping a marker on his head and he looked like he was trying to figure out a strangely complicated graph drawn on a whiteboard before him. Then suddenly his face brightened up like already figured it out and poof! Just like that, he was gone.

And as suddenly as he vanished, I began to put two and two together. She had been the one that set me up for that shoot that gave me the Hives.

She also was the one that called, not Felicia during the party. This also means she sent the email to me. She had known me well enough to know where to hit me, and how I would react. She just set her traps and watched me fall right into them.

Strangely, I was impressed. She knew how to handle her grudges. I just wished she weren't bonkers, then we'd have been soulmates.

"By the foolish look on your pretty face right now, it's obvious you are just putting two and two together," she said, "Painfully, while watching you execute that Con on Felicia I saw that you had all it takes to be one of us."

I suspected that if she wanted me dead I'd be right now, so I said something very foolish "hey!" I croaked "now that we are truly acquainted and I have shown that I am like you in every way...."

I paused and forced a weak sexy smile, ".... Let's finish what we started in that dark room" I continued, but I imagined how stupid I must have looked at that moment, so I lost the smile.

She continued like she hadn't heard me talk at all.

It was as if she was musing loudly "But then... now that I am thinking about it, it wouldn't be that difficult to teach you our ways..." she soliloquized, then she began to smile wickedly like she just came to a realization. She was regarding me intently by this time; like a hawk watched a rabbit.

"Um..." I said, crushed under her intense gaze "what exactly are we turning me to?"

The haze that clouded her face vanished momentarily as she regarded me again, she smiled and said: "A Twenty-first-century witch, of course, weren't you listening to that sermon that day." She paused dramatically "oh wait, you were a little o-CCUP-ied at the moment weren't you" and she laughed –this time in her voice, at her own little pun.

I just stared at her. Surely, she must be kidding, I thought to myself when suddenly I felt the tree I was tied to move, the rope loosened and I fell to the floor, still too weak to support my own weight. Promptly, I witnessed a very graphic lifelike conversion of a tree to a gorgeous woman.

When did she put a VR on me, I thought to myself – I just saw a tree become a grown woman. A dumb part of me thought 'Maybe being a witch wouldn't be so bad after all, they look like they are loaded... that's for sure.'

Then, the nude woman before me began to sing.

I recognized the voice immediately, it was the voice of my mom, it was Toyin's voice, it was the voice of my sister, it was the voice of that teacher I had a crush on in Junior secondary school. It was the voice of Mother Nature.

As she sang other nude female figures began to appear out of thin air. I glanced back at where Nike was clothed and I saw she too had become nude. There was no sign of any discarded clothes, it was as if they just vanished right off her.

Little Jimmy was getting excited. But I ignored that twat, the situation I was in right then was his fault.

All the women before me were gorgeous and naked, fifteen-year-old me will be in heaven right now.

Suddenly, like clockwork, in unison they joined their leader; crooning a lullaby I recognized, the music became air. Air that seconds later filled my lungs made the very core of my being one with the night. I wept at the glory of it, but little Jimmy was starting to get annoying right about then. I could not make him flaccid.

I felt like I was being manipulated by external forces, or maybe it was just the music, but at that point, I was feeling so much pleasure that it began to hurt like a live wire was connected directly to my nether regions.

The pain gradually increased until it became blinding and I could focus on nothing else and then for the third time in this tale 'Out I went, like a light bulb'

PART 4—BELLADONA.

A shrouded figure appeared in the room, it looked very disheveled and had a shocked expression on its face.

The two figures already in the room regarded the new arrival.

The figure called Nightmare said to the new arrival "What happened to you Hallucination? I've been looking all over for you,"

The new arrival replied the figure that addressed him, "Nightmare, where have you been? I had to go in when you were not around,"

"So why are you back and looking like that, you usually take longer than that" the third – and only figure that had not spoken yet, asked suddenly.

Hallucinations gestured towards the center of the room.

***

I woke up lying down on a bed, with a spasm and a roar of pain.

I was in complete agony and I felt something jammed to my crotch, this strange device was the source of my discomfort.

I tried to clear my head and take stock of my surroundings' but the pain made it impossible so I focused my energy on getting the device off my treasures.

I tensed and made to move my body away from contact with the device jammed in my privates, but I encountered restraints that I never felt before – and whoever tied the knots meant business.

My attempts must have alerted this individual that I was awake because I heard a female voice say, "Oh, Alright. You are awake!" The pain seized suddenly.

'Wait a minute,' I thought to myself 'I know that voice…"

Then it began to come back to me including a memory of a ridiculous hallucination that must have been triggered when 'she' knocked me out.

"Pamela!" I said as menacingly as I could muster.

I felt her loosen something in the restraints and suddenly I could move more freely. I wiggled until I was in a position to see her sitting beside me and in her hand I saw the source of my agony – a Taser.

'My God' I thought – 'she woke me up with a Taser' She beamed at me looking batshit crazy and very pretty in a snow-white's evil stepmom sort of way.

I picked up my list of available speeches and began to cross out jokes. I look towards using the calm speech approach, there were lots of those on the list.

Then it hit me, I was in my own room, on my own bed. This felt like a well-planned scheme.

I was stripped down to my underwear and so were my captors.

I heard a grunt beside me and I turned to see Tiny Tim fully dressed and tied to a chair. Standing beside the chair was the girl I saw with him earlier in the house.

Then it all clicked in my brain!

I looked back and forth between the two captors, the resemblance was uncanny, no wonder Pamela had looked familiar when I first met her.

"Oh, I see you've met Sarah," Pamela said. She then slowly shifted her gaze to the Taser. She then raised it and began to move around in mesmerizing whorl motions in front of her, but the show suddenly ended when a hand snatched it from her and jammed it in my ribs.

If I could scream I would have but something told me that would probably make things worse so I bit down my scream and tried hard not to spasm.

The hand belonged to no one but Sarah, I guess insanity ran in the family.

"I've told you sis, do not play with torture devices," Sarah said as she climbed atop the bed with a mischievous bloodthirsty *Ted Bundy* kind smile.

I recognized that smile, and unlike the naïve little idiot in the hallucination, I knew death was a possibility.

In fact, I could feel him in the room with us – lurking in the corners waiting so I chose my next words carefully.

"Hi, uh Sarah, what did, uh Tim do to you?" I asked, trying to ascertain if the reason we were in this mess was because of one of his crazy antics backfiring and I was collateral damage.

She grabbed my arm and suddenly used it to flip me on my butt with a move I have only seen in the movies.

I now faced my friend's position and I could see his face clearly now. When he noticed this, he shook his head once at me.

As soon as I saw this, I knew that none of this was his fault. There were sometimes when we were drunk when we made up non-verbal symbols that we only knew amongst ourselves because Tiny Tim got paranoid when he was inebriated.

That little Headshake meant 'not me'.

Suddenly the guy with the pipe appeared one last time and said: 'In order to defeat your enemy you have to know your enemy' he was dressed as a monk this time; with his hair greyed out. And with these words, he vanished finally.

I understood what he meant. So I said as I felt her place her knee on my back "Why?"

"Because..." Sarah began, then paused and it sounded like she was actually just thinking about why she abducted me and my friend and got us tied down in my own apartment.

She adjusted something in the restraint and the cinch became tighter then she finally suggested "Umm... I don't know all men are scum and we love getting rid of scum?"

Whoa! I thought. She just used the phrase 'Get rid'. I may have flunked high school English but doesn't that phrase mean 'to kill'.

"Ooh, I have one ...." Pamela suddenly piped in "We are CIA spies and we are here .... because Jimmy has been *a bad boy*." The last part she said by mimicking a toddler.

It was clear by now that they just wanted to have fun with me – I was their little plaything, till they probably got bored and moved on to my tiny friend over there.

I felt Sarah lean closer to me then she whispered with a low sultry voice "You really made your way into Santa's naughty list this time haven't you Jimmy boy?"

I could hear genuine pleasure in that voice then suddenly it occurred to me that they might be planning to rape us.

No sooner had this thought left my head when I felt sharp zap right on my spinal column. My whole body jolted and I struggled with my restraints again.

Pamela stood up and reached for something on the floor, it was my trousers. She searched through the pockets for a few seconds and brought out my phone.

"Let's play a game," she said, "Jimmy you love games don't you?"

Sarah suddenly grabbed my hair and lifted my head to face her. "She asked you a question!" she screamed in my face brandishing the Taser menacingly.

I nodded my head when I saw the Taser. I would have done anything to not have that thing touch me again.

"Which game do you want to play Pamela?" Sarah asked her sister.

"Well, a pretty boy like him has got to have a lot of chicks in his contacts!" she said scooting closer so she was beside me, "Well…. The rule of this game is simple…"

"Ooh I know this game," Sarah said, she seemed excited at the prospect of this game "he gets tazed for every girl we see on his contact… right?"

'I am done for' I thought to myself, 'What the heck! There were hundreds of female contacts on my phone.'

"Correct!" she said "Shall we SIS!"

Pamela rubbed her palms together like an ice-cream enthusiast that was about to dive into a bowl of sundae. "Let the games begin!"

On and on for the next thirty minutes they alternated the Taser between eachother. Then they *oohed* and *aahed* when they saw my various reactions – Sounding like cotton candy stuffed kids watching a circus show.

I was in agony and my whole body was sore, I was beginning to understand how Nazi prisoners had felt.

I got a break from the pain when Sarah said "I want to go tinkle, let's give him a break, then we move to the more serious stuff."

Wait a minute? I thought to myself, *this isn't the serious stuff.*

My imagination began to go wild, my gosh! 'I must be in a horror movie' I thought or maybe... just maybe this was just a hallucination inside another hallucination, but the pain seemed real enough.

I heard as she got down from the bed, and her footsteps as they receded in the direction of the bathroom.

Then Pamela suddenly grabbed my head as soon as her sister was out of earshot and suddenly whispered "Or maybe my sister ran into your buddy over there and you are just the very unlucky friend that got wrapped up in a situation you have no reasonable explanation for..."

She paused to let the message sink in and then continued "...think about it, all these feelings of hate you feel towards us right now really should be directed at him, it's all his fault."

She used her hand to force my gaze in the direction of where Tiny Tim was strapped to a wooden chair. "I want you to say it!" she says as she jammed the Taser behind my skull. Pain erupted in my skull and the one I could think of was make it stop.

Then tiny Tim spoke up for the first time.

"Yes! Pamela, it's all my fault please don't hurt my friend anymore."

She lifted the Taser as soon as she heard what he said.

For the first time in thirty minutes, I watched tiny Tim closely and noticed a micro movement that I presumed was for just me.

He continuously ever so slightly tilted his head towards one direction and I followed his gaze to see a pair of eyes peeping from behind the door which was opened a crack.

"We invented this one to point out subtly to the other when we saw a girl with a fat ass in public."

I tried to use my eye to tell him to communicate with our observer. However, I was not sure he understood me at all.

Then came our first stroke of luck that night –Pamela, was a little bit into masochism and it seemed she hid this particular fetish from her partner in crime.

She began to audibly Taser herself as she did a weird dance on top of me. I glanced towards the entrance again and I saw as our spectator now approached the bed slowly.

She was female and she was dressed elegantly. Apart from those two things, I couldn't deduce anything else about the approaching stranger from this distance.

Wait a minute! I thought to myself. I know that gait anywhere. Our newcomer was Toyin!

My heart skipped a beat – she was going to see me like this helpless and shamed. I wanted to tell her to go get help, what the hell was she thinking.

My captor began to make little groans of pain and pleasure, she even snuck one tase in on me and then she closed her eyes resumed her little fetish ritual.

Toyin was upon us at this point, I was very glad to see her. Her presence made the pain on my sore body seem dull and far away. I didn't have time to dwell on this as she suddenly accidentally scuffed her feet on the floor loudly enough to draw Pamela out of the haze of deranged sexual pleasure.

She paused her dance and glanced straight at the door of the toilet when she saw the sound didn't come from that direction.

She was about to look behind her and ruin the surprise when I piped up "I know I should have said this earlier. but fuck! I am going do it now."

She paused what she was about to do and regarded me –my ruse to distract her had worked perfectly. She raised up the taser and put it dangerously close to my chest – that clearly meant choose your next words carefully.

So I clear my throat loudly as Toyin got directly behind her.

Toyin gave me a nod, and I took that to mean start talking so I said: "No, I do not agree with you about Tiny Tim." I paused to see her stunned at my little rebellious statement, she must have thought the threat of the taser was enough to drive away all impetuous thought before they coalesced into words.

Before she recovered however from her mild astonishment, Toyin tackled her from behind stunning her the second time.

She screamed loudly and she began to struggle with Toyin for possession of the taser – it seemed like no one was losing or winning when suddenly the Taser was in Toyin's hands.

She didn't waste any precious time as she began to tase Pamela right on the chest where I heart should be. She continued to hold it there... didn't let up for one second, even when Pamela's jerks became spasms and she began to foam at her mouth, Toyin had a weird faraway look on her face like she was in a trance.

I noticed that if I did nothing, Pamela could die. I watched for a few more seconds and then I could take it no more, so I rolled my intention being to hit Toyin off her but really all I succeeded in doing was jolting her.

The jolt was enough though, she strangely became aware all of sudden and she tossed the Taser away like it had become a snake.

She placed her head in her arms and began to sob. I kept my eye on Toyin, still scared that the incidence would repeat itself as I scooted closer to Pamela so that I could hear if she was still breathing.

Her breathing was shallow but it was still there. I realized I just saved my captor and was feeling like a perfect disciple of Christ when I suddenly heard a scuffle and to see the source was Sarah, she was back from the bathroom, I had been too engrossed in the battle on the bed that I hadn't noticed her approach.

She seemed to have extracted Tiny Tim from the chair, they were both standing a few feet away from the chair – her voluntarily, him not so much. He looked like he was motivated to stay still by the knife she held to his throat and the dildo she jammed deep into his throat.

When she saw that I had already noticed her she said "Smiling Jimmy, what a funny nickname. Infiltrating your life was quite easy, I mean you were smart enough to notice that it was strange for Pig head over here..." she paused slightly to gesture at Tiny Tim "... to bring a girl here twice but in the end, I played the both of you."

Toyin was kneeling beside me now, having stopped sobbing when our other captor made her presence known. She began to untie me but the knots were so intricate that it was taking some time. I decided to keep Sarah talking.

"I don't see it..." I said with a very convincing fake puzzled expression. "...how did you do it – play us both I mean.?" I asked and I hoped she bought it.

I racked my brain for something, anything that could help me out of that situation but all I was drawing was blanks.

"The first time I was in here I stole your father's watch so that I could put a tiny tracker chip in it. I then mailed it back to your friend whom I was sure was gonna return it to you. I then used my exceptional talent on the bed to warp his rigid mind into keeping me around..." she said with a cocky smile. It seemed she was enjoying this way too much.

Something strange happened though, I noticed that Tim's eyes were closed and his mouth was moving ever so slightly –even though it looked very weird with the dildo in his mouth, he seemed to be saying a prayer.

I began to realize what was going through his mind.

"Faster! please!" I silently urged Toyin and she visibly hastened her efforts to get the restraints off me.

"... grabbing your pal was the easy part, I just called him and told him to show up outside the building and he obliged, like the fool he is." Sarah continued obviously too engrossed in recanting her diabolic plan to notice her captive praying.

She jammed the dildo down his throat enough to choke him, then she asked without even looking at him "Aren't you just an old fool?" she made the motion to jam the dildo down again when my friend began to bob his head rigorously to prevent a repeat of the last dildo incident.

I kept on staring at him. His eyes were wide open now there was a slight sadness there. Then he confirmed my suspicion that he was about to do something stupid; He caught my eye and then he grinned and winked twice.

"You see what I mean," she said triumphantly after which kept on rambling but I wasn't listening to her at this point I glanced at my restraint and I saw that Toyin was almost done untying me, but I strangely knew she won't be done in time.

If by now you have guessed that the grin and two winks meant something more, you would be absolu-freakingly surprised that you were right.

The grin meant; I am about to do something stupid, and the winks meant goodbye.

I mouthed a no at him but his attention already shifted.

I began to shrug and wiggle as I tried to get rid of the remaining restraints, it was then that both Toyin and Tim's captor figured out something was wrong, but it was already too late.

I watched as my friend hit his captor with a very sharp elbow jab in her guts, she doubled up but remained standing and in possession of the knife while Tiny Tim slipped out of her grip.

His victory was short lived though as he tripped and fell face down.

Her reaction to this unexpected assault though was perfectly normal, she just calmly went along with it like an experienced fighter would have. She quickly noticed his misstep and with the lunge of someone who knew what she was doing she pounced on him and jabbed him with the knife in the back.

All this happened so fast it looked like I was just watching a scene out the movies.

Puddles of red began to form beneath the still form of my friend on the floor, ironically he held the dildo in his hand like some form of weapon.

This made me recall a night when he told me of a dream he had with a lot of steamy sex and a lot of sex toys. He had ended his narrative that day by saying this "I tell you, if I get to choose how I want to die, I'll tell the angel of death to let me die with a dildo in my hand... Trust me, it is the ultimate weapon" he had the most perverted look on his face when he said that last part.

"The remaining figure in the room amongst the trio that was there before shook his head. He was there that night."

It seemed now that in a strange way he got what he wished for.

Toyin tapped me on the shoulder and pointed out that she was done with the restraints but I was still too stunned by how everything had gone south so fast to move an inch.

Suddenly, I noticed that Sarah was moving again. She stood in one quick fluid motion and began to laugh hysterically as she grabbed the chair and raised it above her head and made to hit Toyin with it.

Immediately, I snapped out of my reverie. I jumped atop her abruptly and tensed but I felt no impact.

Gently and slowly, I slid slowly off Toyin. When I turned around fully I was presented with a very unexpected scene.

I sat at the edge of the bed stunned as I saw tiny Tim looking pale but alive standing over the unmoving form of Sarah. He was holding the dildo in his hand like a makeshift weapon.

From the look of things, she had missed his heart and stabbed him in the shoulder. He must have tripped her and then knocked her out with the dildo while she was concentrating on us.

He was breathing heavily, "See! I told you" he said with a weak smile as he gestured at the dildo.

I just laughed and said "Yea, I see you were right"

He looked as if he could barely keep himself upright at this point. I rushed over to his side to support him and got no resistance. "I am glad you alive Tiny Tim, but do you know anybody that can keep it that way?" I asked.

His eyelids were drooping at this point so I shook him till he looked a bit more aware and then I repeated myself, "Do you know anyone we could call that can help treat you or keep you alive till we get to a hospital?"

He was still unresponsive so I turned to Toyin who had been silently watching us up till this point and said "hey... how about you? Know any nurses or doctors" she shook her head and said "the ones I know stay very far away and wouldn't get here in time."

"Fuck!" I cussed, I was about to attempt another trick to try to keep him awake when he suddenly jolted awake like an electric shock had just run up his spine, I turned to see Toyin holding the knife stuck to his back. "Hey, stop that!" I shouted as I tried to interrupt whatever the hell she was doing.

She just shifted back when she saw I didn't like what she was doing one bit. Her trick though seemed to work like a charm, my friend was beginning to notice us again.

"Pick my phone from my back pocket..." he breathed out after he caught his breath "and dial this phone number." He then went on to dictate a phone number to me. I dialed the number and it began to ring.

I could tell that this call had woken its recipient up by the way she answered the phone "This better be worth it" I heard her say right off the bat.

Tim gestured that I should place the receiver closer to his mouth so he could talk to her. "Hey peaches its corndog," he said "I need your help…"

"Corny!" the voice exclaimed in a way cheerier tone than her last. "What happened?!"

"…I am injured and bleeding out in my best friend's apartment. Could you arrange something please?"

"… I am on my way don't you dare die on me!" she said and the call ended abruptly.

***

Twenty minutes later we were all in the parking lot.

Tiny Tim was on a trolley being wheeled off to the hospital.

They had arrived exactly thirty minutes after we made that call so don't be impressed our medical sector still sucked.

Myself and Toyin had to lug him out of the building ourselves.

They had stabilized him and waited until a short pretty adult lady – the lady from the phone I presumed, arrived, after which she immediately rushed to his side and snapped some commands at the paramedics and they wheeled him off.

It seemed we were in the early hours of the morning so early that the moon still provided what little illumination was to be seen.

She barked some commands at the police officers that had arrived with her and gestured in our direction. *'Whoa,'* I thought to myself *'that doesn't seem like a good sign'* Toyin noticed me tense and said; "Don't worry, she just told those dudes to do whatever we want for us till she came back."

I turned to look at her again with a puzzled look and asked: "How in the hell can you tell all that from over here?"

She just shrugged and said "I read lips" like it was a normal thing that every human being on this earth did.

"Whoa, that's cool." I said, "how did you come to be in my house by the way?" I asked her.

The adult lady had gotten into the ambulance and it was already zooming off. The two policemen she had just finished addressing approached and got to us in time to hear Toyin recant her story.

"I was leaving the party when I saw Tiny Tim leaving in a rush, I got to my car to see that his car was still in the parking lot. I turned to check if I had passed him on the way down but that was unlikely, he was just ahead of me..."

Her story got interrupted as a black Volvo pulled up and I was surprised to see Ajayi and Andrew alight the vehicle.

I regarded them as they approached and thought of how weird a night this had been. I glanced at Toyin, she looked as pretty as ever even with all that had happened.

Andrew was first to speak "Can someone pleaaassse tell me why we passed an ambulance on the way here?" he said, "Jimmy! what the heck is going on!?"

"I have no idea... just trying to figure it out myself," I said, "Hello Ajayi, what a coincidence that you chose today to show up?"

At this point, I noticed that the cops were questioning Toyin.

"Hi Jimmy. Coincidence has nothing to do with it..." he replied "but it seems your tale far surpasses mine" he says gesturing at the uniformed officers.

"Yea I had a rough night," I said

Andrew was staring gape-mouthed at the cops as they talked to Toyin. "Jimmy, please tell me that ambulance had nothing to do with what is going on here." He said.

"Well, it had Tiny Tim in it... so yeah, it kinda does." I replied.

Ajayi raised an eyebrow at this. So I said to enunciate "A friend of ours..."

Then he had that oh expression like he understood.

Andy looked stunned, "I swear to Interruptus, if you don't start talking right now… I might lose it." He said.

So I rushed over the tale as quickly as I could, I embellished a teeny bit though by telling them it took both of them to knock me out. By the time I was done Andrew was glancing up at our apartment.

"Wait a minute, they are both up there right now?"

I nodded

"Damn it… dude, what if they woke up?" he said.

"Don't worry our girl over there…" I said, tilting my head towards Toyin "…tied them up nice – gave them a little piece of their own medicine."

"Oh, in that case, can I see them?" he said talking to the cops who had finished questioning Toyin long enough for them to hear part of my story.

The taller and apparently more superior of the two shrugged, like it didn't matter and said: "Our orders are to secure them till opening hours when our superiors can book them."

"Who was that lady that gave the order, sir?" I asked him.

"I thought you knew…" said the officer "we all just refer to her as the woman or the lady – she is a very scary woman and she referred to your friend as her husband."

"Husband...?" I and Andrew echoed, we both had disbelieving looks on our faces.

Ajayi who had been watching silently suddenly said "Oh... you mean – the mistress" like he knew who he was referring to.

"You are not wrong sir; she really is scary. Met her once.... It was not a pleasant experience." He continued.

Toyin nodded too like she too knew this *mistress, lady whatever* individual.

"Slow down... scary how?" I asked

Andrew nodded like he too wanted to know.

"Well, it's hard to explain..." Ajayi said, "You have to experience yourself to understand.

"Well... is she a cop, politician, crime boss...?" Andrew asked.

Ajayi shrugged like he too had no idea and everyone turned to look at the officers. "Don't look at me, I don't know too..." the officer that spoke before said "...all I know is that my superior's superiors follow her order like she is the devil's spouse."

Toyin came over to my side and said "I am going up to show them where we got them tied up," she placed her palms on my cheek then continued "you don't have to come along, I noticed you wincing when we were carrying Tiny Tim down the stairs."

I smiled and placed my palms on top of hers "Thanks, Toyin. You are just amazing."

Everyone but I and Ajayi went up to the apartment.

He was silent for about twenty minutes leaving me to my thoughts.

"You've had quite the experience, Jimmy," he broke the silence. "I actually called yesterday that I was going to swing by your place."

"Oh, when was that?" I asked trying to recall if I saw any missed call from him.

I didn't so I said "you know what forget it... what brings you here?"

"Well... it seems fickle right now but I was worried about you... something just felt wrong about that girl I talked to over the phone when we last spoke – the one with the issues with the crime lord." He said.

"Oh..." I said my face lighting up "you mean Toyin?"

Ajayi suddenly froze and said "Toyin – your assistant was the one I spoke to that day?" he asked tensely. He looked like I guess I would look if I learnt that peanuts caused cancer (Something I like to refer to as the ghosts exist expression).

"Yea...What's the matter with that?" I said, I was worried because of the way he looked.

"Wait here..." he said.

He made to run into the building but I grabbed him before he could move and said "Explain! Right now!"

He paused and glanced at my hands grabbing his arm. I knew he could have thrown me or twisted my arms but he decided to try the calm approach.

"Well, I visited that criminal dude, the one she mentioned – actually I was in prison for some other reason but I saw him and I figured why not talk to him." He said gently removing my fingers from his arm.

"and..." I said with my heart in my mouth.

"She lied Jimmy... he had no idea what I was saying when I confronted him" Ajayi said finally "I know what you're thinking... and I checked, she lied. And right now she is up there with your friend and her accomplices!"

I stood dumbfounded, not drawing breath, just staring. There was a riot in my brain, my mind was trying to come to terms with what I just heard. This was worse that the extinction of peanuts—this was worse than anything!

Ajayi turned to go into the building but stopped and asked me "Is there any shorter way to your apartment?"

I heard him but I was still too shocked to process what he said.

"Jimmy! Snap out of it, I need you." He said tapping me incessantly till I responded.

"Oh, we can use the faulty stairs, it's shorter," I said still dazed.

"Show me," he said and he gestured for me to lead the way.

I lead the way, firstly by jogging slowly but Ajayi urged me from behind to move faster so it became an all-out run.

We climbed the wooden stairs in twos, the floorboards creaking as we ran as fast as we could. I recognized a particular stair as the one that was faulty and skipped it.

I halted and turned to warn Ajayi but he was right behind me so I was too late. The stair came loose and Ajayi stumbled but I quickly grabbed him before he rolled down and I assisted him to find his balance.

"Damn... that was close," he said as he caught his breath.

We started to move again, this time with more caution though and arrived at the apartment soon after that.

The door was ajar and the place was strangely quiet.

I looked at Ajayi, I knew he wanted me to stay back but we were in this together – I needed answers.

I made to go in but he barred my way and whispered "Let me go in first."

He entered and I heard a short struggle, as I heard this I rushed into the apartment jumping over an unconscious cop I hadn't seen a moment before.

I glanced around and saw Ajayi in the living room holding the Taser. He must have snatched from either Sarah or Pamela, it seemed like they had tried to ambush him but he had gotten the upper hand since he expected it.

His stance was one of someone who has been in fights frequently, almost like Shifu.

Sarah held aloft over her head one of the cop's batons. Her sister held a knife she was standing on top of the couch opposite her sister.

Sarah swung the baton at Ajayi's head but he was quick and he dodged it bowing low and with a quick jerk movement he stabbed the Taser into her gut. She gasped but despite the pain went at him with the baton again.

While this was going on Pamela noticed my entrance and exclaimed in Victorian English "Jimmy Boy!"

"Pamela…" I said and I looked to the side to see a trail of blood lead to the other officer –sitting and leaning on the wall pale from blood loss.

"… your handiwork I presume?" I asked gesturing at the officer.

She actually blushed and said "No…," she said and she pointed in the direction of the kitchen "it's all her…"

I checked and didn't see Andrew anywhere in view, I raised my hands and approached the couch and said to Pamela "We can end this without violence…" I said, "just tell me how much she paid you, I could double it."

She jumped down from the couch crazy and giddy as ever and said "What is it… Jimmy boy… Are you scared?" she asked making a pouty face.

I heard a stumble and I noticed that Ajayi had succeeded in overpowering Sarah. She was lying face flat, he held her hands behind her with one hand and placed his knee on her back. His other hand held the baton and the Taser.

He tossed me the baton to me and brought the Taser menacingly close to her face as she struggled and said "Enough!"

Pamela stared at her defeated sister and then me as I approached with the baton. "You know what?" she said as she looked at her sister "Sorry sis, but I am done with this shit.... She didn't pay us enough for all this shit... Bye Jimmy boy" and she sauntered out of the apartment.

I watched her go and thought 'Thank God'. I wasn't sure I could take her.

I had my back to the apartment door and I was checking to see if the policeman was still alive when I suddenly heard Ajayi scream "Duck!" not a second later I was flat on the floor.

I heard a thud sound and a second later Pamela's voice "Oops!" she said and then I heard the door slam.

Slowly I rose up to see she had thrown the knife at me but had missed totally and hit the cop in the chest instead. I checked to see she really was gone this time.

I gazed at the lifeless corpse in front of me and I almost lost it. He stared and saw nothing – he really was dead!

"Deep breaths." I heard someone say but a red haze began to fill my vision and rage erased my panic attack.

I turned in the direction of the kitchen and I stormed in there with the baton in my hand.

I saw Toyin sitting beside an unconscious Andy, she was playing with a lighter. They were on the floor opposite the sink.

She glanced at me for a second then went back to staring dumbly at the lighter. There was a strange smell in the kitchen.

I racked my brain for where I had perceived that smell before but I couldn't place it.

"Toyin!" I said as I approached her. I noticed the smell got stronger the closer I got —suddenly I figured it out.

It was the smell of cooking gas, and it was very strong. I halted my steps and stared at the lighter in her hands. I was a few feet from her by this time.

She noticed that I had stopped my approach, "I didn't want it to get this far..." she muttered almost like she was talking to herself. "None of this would have happened if you had not kissed her..."

Kissed who? I thought, then suddenly I realized that she must have been right there in the shadows – watching.

She turned to the obviously unconscious Andrew and said "... he kissed her... he kissed her" she suddenly paused like she noticed it was strange he wasn't responding. She balled up her fists and pounded them on his stomach continuously as she said "He kissed her!... kissed her!" he groaned but did not wake up.

I dropped the baton and winced as she began pounding on my friend, his fiancée will kill me if anything happened to him.

"Hey! Toyin..." I said gently but firmly so that I could cut through the insanity.

She stopped hurting my friend and looked at me again but I saw a little Lucidity this time so I tried my luck.

"Honey... it's me you want, please! Stop hitting my friend." I said.

She smiled and stood up, "Jimmy..." she said like she was really just seeing me in the kitchen. "What have we done?" she asked.

"Toyin... I ...." I said but lumps in my throat did not let me finish the sentence.

I noticed Andrew stirring so I decided to get her out of there quickly.

I suddenly found my courage, my survival instinct kicked it out of the corner it was hiding in.

"Toyin, I remember the day we met.... You see, I have a lousy memory when it comes to recalling the past..." I began "but that particular day I don't think I can ever forget, you turned my life upside down – I was hooked right the second I laid my eyes on you. You were like a little star that wandered off course and landed in my little galaxy and shine you did. Your glow was so astounding that even other galaxies in my universe felt the warmth you brought to my life..."

She stared at me astounded, I began to inch closer to her one step after the other as I continued talking "...but like they say give a doctor a pencil and an architect a scalpel suddenly they are no longer professionals but dumbass fucks. I was an architect with a scalpel trying to understand what the fuck love was."

I was directly in front of her as I said this.

"I was a fool and I am sorry, now I know what it is truly to love. I love you Toyin!" I said as I grabbed and kissed her.

She tasted like *belladonna.* So sweet was the poison that was her lips.

Out of the corner of my eye, I saw Ajayi lurking at the entrance of the kitchen, he was crouched low and was beckoning to the now conscious Andrew.

"But... but...." She blurted abruptly as she broke the kiss off "I..."

But I cut her off by kissing her again.

I checked again to see Andrew crawling towards where Ajayi was.

Ajayi must have told him to do that...smart thinking. I thought.

I turned her around as my hand began to explore her various curves and mounds.

Mounds that had given me sleepless nights... curves that plagued my nightmares.

I pushed her against the cooker as I felt her raise her palms up to my face and I heard a clink as the lighter dropped from her hands.

We both began to breathe heavily, our hands became explorers – Christopher Columbus our mentor, roaming and discovering new wonders on the other's body.

I grabbed her butt and I felt her freeze, she suddenly shoved me away and I fell backward to the floor.

"I saw you..." she said looking down at me as her eyes began to cloud over gradually "...this means nothing to you...? women mean nothing to you! You are a liar... and you deserve to burn!" her voice rising in volume with every word.

She suddenly went for the lighter but I was quicker and I shoved it far away with my foot.

I never saw her foot coming though... right up till the point that it performed a short experiment of inelastic collision with my crotch.

I grunted and doubled over.

I groaned in agony as I heard sounds of pans colliding as she rummaged through the kitchen utensils on the cabinet behind her. I guess she was looking for something to light the whole place up with.

I grabbed her foot and used it to pull her away from the cabinet. She stumbled and fell atop me such that she was straddling me and she was not alone, she had a huge frying pan in her hand.

She raised it as if to smash my head but she paused for a few seconds – that was all the time I needed though.

Survival instinct went gung-ho! And kicked fatigue to the curb as I summoned what little strength I had that had not been zapped or pounded out of me as I grabbed her around the waist and tossed her as far as I could.

I guess I didn't know my own strength as she crashed through the door that led to the balcony and crashed into the chairs there. There she lay sprawled, gazing upwards and breathing heavily.

I could see the sun barely peeping out of the clouds as I struggled to get to my feet. I ignored her as I found the source of the leak and twisted a knob to cut off the leak. The smell of the gas was now so strong it made me nauseous.

After this, I approached her, she was sitting up at this point and she had a smile on her face.

I thought she would look horrible but she looked like she was posing for the cover of a magazine.

"Jimmy..." she said testing the word out. That was the first time I ever heard her call me that.

I paused at the door and studied her – she seemed lucid again and strangely calm.

"Jimmy boy... Smiling Jimmy..." she said those names rolling off her lips "I am crazy about you," she said,

She began to get up, I let her. I felt eyes and I saw both Andrew and Ajayi standing in the kitchen behind me.

When she was barely upright, her feet wobbling like it was a struggle for her, I knew it was over.

She had a very sad smile on her face. "Did you mean it...?" she said "What you said before...? You've really felt that way about me... all this while?"

I shook my head "I did Toyin!" I said "...unfortunately stars' burnout!"

"James...!" I heard Ajayi say behind me suddenly. I looked back to see him gesturing vigorously in her direction.

I turned back just in time to see her move, she leaped atop the railing of the balcony.

She had been faking her weakness because she made for the railing of the balcony in a sudden burst of speed, I reached for her but I was a fraction of a second late. She grabbed the metal railing and lofted herself so that she was directly atop it. She risked a quick glance back at me and then she jumped.

I dived for her and caught *it*...

I caught the *look on her face* as she fell and it threw shivers into my spines anew. She seemed happy and contented.

I felt the guys join me as we watched blood pool under her on the floor below.

I looked around to see we had an audience, people were peeping from their windows and some even came out to investigate what the noise was all about.

"I guess she really wanted to burn out," Ajayi said as he placed a hand on my shoulder.

I glanced at him sadly and replied: "No... she believed she loved me so much that she had to protect me from herself..."

I didn't know how I knew this but I was fairly certain I was right.

"... in the end it was an inner battle...; a deranged Toyin versus a Toyin that was weirdly so in love with me she was willing to die for me." I finished.

Sirens wailed in the distances and the tardy sun was no more hiding behind the clouds.

I felt Andrew who still looked a little pale place his hands across my shoulders and he said finally "Let's get outta here"

"I couldn't agree more." Ajayi said.

***

AJAYI'S EPILOGUE—
TRANSCEDENCE

I stood in front of the mirror beside the door and gnawed on a chocolate bar.

I checked out my shirt and I saw that it had a little rip. *It must have ripped during that little fiasco yesterday* – I thought.

I glanced around the apartment trying to ascertain if I missed any detail when I heard a knock at the door.

Of course, I knew who it was – they were here because I called them.

It was the police.

They knocked again and announced out loud "Police!"

I considered opening the door for them and dismissed it – serves them right for making me wait this long.

It had been a pretty normal day for me. I had woken up, brushed my teeth, worn the same shirt I wore the day before to Jimmy's and of course tracked down Toyin's apartment.

Finding the apartment had been a little more frustrating than I anticipated. I was pretty sure it would have taken our *'friends'* outside at least a week to find this place though.

I texted them an hour and a half ago and they were just showing up. I actually had my money on an hour but they must have been feeling especially tardy today.

I heard a familiar female voice say suddenly "Break it!"

That's strange, I thought

Quickly I glanced through the peephole and saw the *lady* from yesterday– I knew the voice sounded familiar. By the *lady,* I meant a short ass looking woman that happens to scare the heck out of me with good reason.

I saw the six cops outside the door with her, scrambling to obey her order. I suspected that they were going to kick the door down.

I unlocked the door with a loud click and returned to the mirror to check my teeth for chocolate flakes as I pocketed what was left of the chocolate.

I heard as *seal team six* outside scrambled for their weapons but the woman just barged in and had her first look of the place.

I watched her take it all in as she noticed me by the side picking at my teeth, her expression was a perfect carbon copy of mine when I just got here.

The place was as pristine as a surgical theatre, not a single thing was out of place in the whole apartment.

Usually, when you had a case of insanity it was the opposite, but Toyin was no ordinary psychopath.

"Samuel Ajayi..." she said finally as her companions slipped into the house.

The District commanding officer, the only one amongst them that had a government-issued pistol had his gun out of its holster and heaved an obvious sigh when he saw it was just me.

I said "Took you long enough" addressing them all.

She yelled to the officers who were still glancing around dumbly like tourists "Well, what are you waiting for! Start from the bedroom."

The five uniformed officers scampered in the presumed direction of the bedroom as she walked up to me and said "...Still up to mischief, I see."

"Well... what else you expect from your favorite God-Brother?" I asked her.

The DCO who was still wandering around the living room suddenly piped up from the front of the shelf he was staring at dumbly. "I sure expected this place to be much of a mess, but what is this? ...It looks like a library threw up in here."

"Well, Sir..." I said, "...if you looked more closely you will see that those are recorded episodes of the soap opera 'My Hero MY LOVE' cataloged by release date."

"You mean that TV show with that pretty actress..." he said "... my wife loves that show!"

I smiled "Yea... that about narrows it down, a TV show with a pretty actress."

I don't think he heard the sarcasm in my voice but he did purse his lips like he wasn't used to being talked to like that.

We suddenly heard a crash from the bedroom.

She winced and said "Ganiyu... go and check on those boys?" Ganiyu nodded and went to check up on his boys.

"Amateurs..." I muttered to myself as I walked to the dining and pulled out two chairs – one a bit farther from the other than necessary.

I waited until she sat before I sat, she scared me that much.

I didn't expect someone of her importance to show up but I guessed for her it was personal.

"Tell me everything," she said as she sat.

I paused and took note of the look on her face. She knew the rules, there was no such thing as favors. I could very much stand up and walk out the door right now without telling her a single word but I chose to stay.

One never knew when a favor from *the mistress* herself could come in handy.

So I did, I told her *everything*.

I told her of the store in the kitchen, I told her of the portraits of Jimmy plastered on every open surface there.

I told her of the accident and the addiction. I told of countless nights of soap operas and loneliness – of how they became her lover and her heroes, medication her popcorn.

Finally, I told her of the plan to fuse reality and fiction. I spewed the bittersweet tales of how Oluwatoyin Adelaja planned to become her lover's hero and transcend to lover.

She was the perfect listener never interrupting me for once, the only sounds present was that of Ganiyu and two other officers scrambling around *wasting their time.*

ABOUT AUTHOR

ONALEYE PELUMI FAVOUR is a fiction writer currently studying Architecture at the Obafemi Awolowo University (OAU), Ile-Ife.

He hails from Oyo state, Nigeria and he writes under the pseudonym 'Fapelo' an alias he coined from a combination of his names (FAvour-PELumi-Onaleye). Though only taking writing seriously a few years ago, there are very few things he loves do more than write.